A BOTANICAL NIGHTMARE

THE LITERARY VAMPIRE SERIES

Edited by
Tom English

DEAD LETTER PRESS
NEW KENT, VA

The Literary Vampire Series, Volume 1:
A BOTANICAL NIGHTMARE
First published 2006 by **DEAD LETTER PRESS**

This edition © 2015

Cover illustration © Allen Koszowski 2015
"A Botanical Nightmare" © Tom English 2015

"The Man-Eating Tree" [1881] by Phil Robinson first published in *Under the Punkah*; London: Sampson Low, 1881.

"The Flowering of the Strange Orchid" [1894] by H. G. Wells first published in the *Pall Mall Budget*, Aug 2, 1894; London: Routledge, 1894.

"The Story of the Grey House" [1898] by E. & H. Heron first appeared in *Pearson's Magazine*, May 1898; London: C. Arthur Pearson, 1898.

"The Purple Terror" [1899] by Fred M. White first published in *The Strand*, Sep 1899; London: George Newnes, 1899.

"The Pavilion" [1915] by Edith Nesbit first published in *The Strand*, Nov 1915; London: George Newnes, 1915.

"The Sumach" [1919] by Ulric Daubeny first published in *The Elemental*; London: Routledge, 1919.

Dead Letter Press makes every effort to obtain permission for use of copyright material. Any omission of copyright attribution is entirely unintentional. If notified, the publisher will make any necessary corrections at the earliest opportunity.

Printed in the United States of America

ISBN-10: 0979633583
ISBN-13: 978-0979633584

REVISED SECOND EDITION
JUNE 2015

DEAD LETTER PRESS
WWW.DEADLETTERPRESS.COM

CONTENTS

A Botanical Nightmare

From sentient trees to body-snatching seed pods, from man-eating flowers to deadly spores, killer plants have been the subject of weird fiction for almost two centuries. They have sprouted in films ranging from Howard Hawks "The Thing" (1951) to Roger Corman's 1961 dark comedy "The Little Shop of Horrors." In fact, so familiar is the idea, that it has become ripe for parody in such works as the cult film "Attack of the Killer Tomatoes."

But the "green menace" did not take root as a distinct weird genre until a handful of writers began to see it as a viable offshoot of the vampire tale. Inspired by the existence of such carnivorous plants as the Venus Flytrap and the Pitcher-plant, they concocted tales of beguiling orchids and bloodthirsty vines.

The first of these stories was Phil Robinson's 1881 tale "The Man-Eating Tree." Philip Stewart Robinson (1847-1902) was both a naturalist and author of several pioneering volumes of Anglo-Indian literature, including *Tigers at Large* and *The Valley of Teetotum Trees*. He was born in India, where he spent his early career before taking a position on the London *Daily Telegraph*. In the early 1880s he travelled throughout Egypt as a war correspondent. In 1898, Robinson also covered the Spanish-American War in Cuba for the Associated Press. That war provides the backdrop for Fred M. White's "The Purple Terror" (1899)

Frederick Merrick White (1859-1930) was a popular British writer of crime thrillers. He wrote more than seventy-five novels with titles such as *The Crimson Blind* (1905), *The Four Fingers* (1908), *The Man Who Was Two* (1922) and *The Devil's Advocate* (1930). White also wrote several science fiction short stories that appeared in *The Strand* and *Pearson's Magazine*. With such convincing tales as "The Invisible Force" and "The Dust of Death" (both 1903), he proved himself a capable rival of one of the founding fathers of SF, H.G. Wells.

Although best known for the SF classics *The War of the Worlds* (1898) and *The Time Machine* (1895), Herbert George Wells (1866-1946) wrote over a dozen classic horror stories, including "The Valley of the Spiders" (1903), "Pollock and the Porroh Man" (1895), and his entry in the vampire plant sub-genre, "The Flowering of the Strange Orchid" (1894). Wells was also an outspoken socialist, and many of his works are notable for their political commentary.

In 1915, Edith Nesbit (1858-1924) published the haunting tale "The Pavilion." Nesbit is remembered today more for her children's books, *The Railway Children* (1904) and *The Enchanted Castle* (1908) among others. But the British writer also penned over two-dozen horror stories, masking her sex under the pseudonyms E. Nesbit and E. Bland. Perhaps the finest of these weird shorts is the frequently reprinted "Man-Size in Marble" (1886).

The most unusual entry in the carnivorous plant genre—and an excellent vampire tale—is Ulric Evan Daubeny's 1919 tale "The Sumach." Daubeny (1888-1922) was a notable antiquarian scholar in the mode of M. R. James. Like James, he had an impressive knowledge of a variety of antiquarian subjects. His scholarly works include *Ancient Cotswold Churches* (1921) and *Orchestral Wind Instruments, Ancient and Modern* (1920). And like James, he was a fine writer of ghost stories. Daubeny's "The Sumach" is even reminiscent of one of James' best tales!

An additional tale is included in this revised edition of *A Botanical Nightmare*, E. & H. Heron's "The Story of the Grey House" (1899) —one of several supernatural tales that featured literature's first psychic detective, Flaxman Low. Low was the creation of Hesketh Vernon Prichard and his mother, Kate. Major Hesketh Prichard (1876-1922) was a soldier, big game hunter and explorer, as well as an expert marksman and cricketer. During the First World War, he introduced measures to counter the threat of German snipers—measures that were credited for saving the lives of over three thousand Allied soldiers. His mother, Kate (1852-1935) was a successful writer whose novel *Don Q's Love Story* was adapted to film, as *Don Q Son of Zorro* (1925).

Read these stories on a stormy night, while the limb of an old elm scratches at the window, and you may need to remind yourself that plants are incapable of evil—that the lovely but lethal orchids, the blood-sucking vines and the man-eating trees in these six tales couldn't possibly thrive in our enlightened world. Keep telling yourself that such things can only exist in a botanical nightmare.

Tom English
New Kent, VA

Tom English is an environmental chemist who enjoys writing weird stuff. His stories have appeared in several print anthologies including Challenger Unbound *(KnightWatch Press, 2015),* Gaslight Arcanum: Uncanny Tales of Sherlock Holmes *(Edge SF and Fantasy) and* Dead Souls *(Morrigan Books). Tom also edited the mammoth* Bound for Evil: Curious Tales of Books Gone Bad, *a 2008 Shirley Jackson Award finalist for best anthology. He resides with his wife, Wilma, surrounded by books and beasts, deep in the woods of New Kent, Virginia.*

"The Man-Eating Tree" first appeared in Robinson's collection Under the Punkah *(London: Sampson Low, 1881). It is the earliest known example of the vampire plant tale. Philip Stewart Robinson (1847-1902) was an accomplished author and journalist and a leading naturalist. In 1893, he wrote on the more traditional variety of bloodsucker, in "The Last of the Vampires."*

THE MAN-EATING TREE

PHIL ROBINSON

[Before committing this paper to the ridicule of the Great Mediocre—for many, I fear, will be inclined to regard this story as incredible—I would venture on the expression of an opinion regarding credulity, which I do not remember to have met before. It is this. Placing supreme Wisdom and supreme Unwisdom at the two extremes, and myself in the exact mean between them, I am surprised to find that, whether I travel towards the one extreme or the other, the credulity of those I meet increases. To put it as a paradox—*whether a man be foolisher or wiser than I am, he is more credulous.* I make this remark to point out to those of the Great Mediocre, whose notice it may have escaped, that credulity is not of itself shameful or contemptible, and that it depends upon the manner rather than the matter of their belief, whether they gravitate towards the sage or the reverse way. According, therefore, to the incredibility found in the following, the reader may measure, as pleases him, his wisdom or his unwisdom. —Z. Oriel]

PEREGRINE ORIEL, MY MATERNAL UNCLE, was a great traveller, as his prophetical sponsors at the font seemed to have guessed he would be. Indeed he had rummaged in the garrets and cellars of the earth with something more than ordinary diligence. But in the narrative of his travels he did not, unfortunately, preserve the judicious caution of Xenophon between the thing seen and the thing heard, and thus it came about that the town-councillors of Brunsbüttel (to whom he had shown a duck-billed platypus, caught alive by him in Australia, and who had him posted for an importer of artificial vermin) were not alone in their scepticism of some of the old man's tales.

Thus, for instance, who could hear and believe the tale of the man-sucking tree from which he had barely escaped with life? He called it himself more terrible than the Upas. "This awful plant, that rears its splendid death-shade in the central solitude of a Nubian fern forest, sickens by its unwholesome humors all vegetation from its immediate vicinity, and feeds upon the wild beasts that, in the terror of the chase, or the heat of noon, seek the thick shelter of its boughs; upon the birds that, flitting across the open space, come within the charmed circle of its power, or innocently refresh themselves from the cups of its great waxen flowers; upon even man himself when, an infrequent prey, the savage seeks its asylum in the storm, or turns from the harsh foot-wounding sword-grass of the glade, to pluck the wondrous fruit that hang plumb down among the wondrous foliage." And such fruit!—"glorious golden ovals, great honey drops, swelling by their own weight into pear-shaped translucencies. The foliage glistens with a strange dew, that all day long drips on to the ground below; nurturing a rank growth of grasses, which shoot up in places so high that their spikes of fierce blood-fed green show far up among the deep-tinted foliage of the terrible tree, and, like a jealous body-guard, keep concealed the fearful secret of the charnel-house within, and draw round the black roots of the murderous plant a decent screen of living green."

Such was his description of the plant; and the other day, looking it up in a botanical dictionary, I find that there is really known to naturalists a family of carnivorous plants; but I see that they are most of them very small, and prey upon little insects only. My maternal uncle, however, knew nothing of this, for he died before the days of the discovery of the sun, dew, and pitcher plants; and grounding his knowledge of the man-sucking tree simply on his own terrible experience of it, explained its existence by theories of his own. Denying the fixity of all the laws of nature except one, that the stronger shall endeavor to consume the weaker, and holding even this fixity to be itself only a means to a greater general changefulness, he argued that—since any partial distribution of the faculty of self-defence would presume an unworthy partiality in the Creator, and since the sensual instincts of beast and vegetable are manifestly analogous—the world must be as percipient as sentient throughout. Carrying on his theory (for it was something more than hypothesis with him) a stage or two further, he arrived at the belief that, given the necessity of any imminent danger or urgent self-interest, every animal or vegetable could eventually revolutionize its nature, the wolf feeding on grass or nesting in trees, and the violet arming herself with thorns or entrapping insects.

"How," he would ask, "can we claim for man the consequence of perceptions to sensations, and yet deny to beasts that hear, see, feel, smell, and taste, a percipient principle co-existent with their senses? And if in the whole range of the animate world there is this gift of self-defence against extirpation, and offence against weakness, why is the inanimate world, holding as fierce a struggle for existence as the other, to be left defenceless and unarmed? And I deny that it is. The Brazilian epiphyte strangles the tree and sucks out its juices.   The tree, again, to starve off its vampire parasite, withdraws its juices into its roots, and piercing the ground in some new place, turns the current of its sap into other growths. The epiphyte then drops off the dead boughs on to the fresh green sprouts springing from the ground beneath it, —and so the fight goes on. Again, look at the Indian peepul tree; in what does the fierce yearning of its roots towards the distant well differ from the sad struggling of the camel to the oasis, or of Sennacherib's army to the saving Nile?

"Is the sensitive plant unconscious! I have walked for miles through plains of it, and watched, till the watching almost made me afraid lest the plant should pluck up courage and turn upon me, the green carpet paling into silver gray before my feet, and fainting away all round me as I walked. So strangely did I feel the influence of this universal aversion, that I would have argued with the plant; but what was the use? If only I stretched out my hands, the mere shadow of the limb terrified the vegetable to sickness; shrubs crumbled up at every commencement of my speech; and at my periods, great sturdy-looking bushes, to whose robustness I had foolishly appealed, sank in pallid supplication. Not a leaf would keep me company. A breath went forth from me that sickened life. My mere presence paralyzed life, and I was glad at last to come out among a less timid vegetation, and to feel the resentful speargrass retaliating on the heedlessness that would have crushed it. The vegetable world, however, has its revenges. You may keep the guinea-pig in a hutch, but how will you pet the basilisk? The little sensitive plant in your garden amuses your children (who will find pleasure also in seeing cockchafers spin round on a pin), but how could you transplant a vegetable that seizes the running deer, strikes down the passing bird, and once taking hold of him, sucks the carcass of man himself, till his matter becomes as vague as his mind, and all his animate capabilities cannot snatch him from the terrible embrace of—God help him! —an inanimate tree?

"Many years ago," said my uncle, "I turned my restless steps towards Central Africa, and made the journey from where the Senegal empties itself into the Atlantic to the Nile, skirting the Great Desert, and reaching Nubia on my way to the eastern coast. I had with me then three native attendants,—two of them brothers, the third, Otona, a young savage from the gaboon uplands, a mere lad in his teens; and one day, leaving my mule with the two men, who were pitching my tent for the night, I went on with my gun, the boy accompanying me, towards a fern forest, which I saw in the near distance. As I approached it I found the forest was cut into two by a wide glade; and seeing a small herd of the common antelope, an excellent beast in the pot, browsing their way along the shaded side, I crept after them. Though ignorant of their real danger the herd was suspicious, and, slowly trotting along before me, enticed me for a mile or more along the verge of the fern growths. Turning a corner I suddenly became aware of a solitary tree growing in the middle of the glade—one tree alone. It struck me at once that I had never seen a tree exactly like it before; but, being intent upon venison for my supper, I looked at it only long enough to satisfy my first surprise at seeing a single plant of such rich growth flourishing luxuriantly in a spot where only the harsh fern-canes seemed to thrive.

"The deer meanwhile were midway between me and the tree, and looking at them I saw they were going to cross the glade. Exactly opposite them was an opening in the forest, in which I should certainly have lost my supper; so I fired into the middle of the family as they were filing before me. I hit a young fawn, and the rest of the herd, wheeling round in their sudden terror, made off in the direction of the tree, leaving the fawn struggling on the ground. Otona, the boy, ran forward at my order to secure it, but the little creature seeing him coming, attempted to follow its comrades, and at a fair pace held on their course. The herd had meanwhile reached the tree, but suddenly, instead of passing under it, swerved in their career, and swept round it at some yards distance.

"*Was I mad, or did the plant really try to catch the deer?* On a sudden I saw, or thought I saw, the tree violently agitated, and while the ferns all round were standing motionless in the dead evening air, its boughs were swayed by some sudden gust towards the herd, and swept, in the force of their impulse, almost to the ground. I drew my hand across my eyes, closed them for a moment, and looked again. The tree was as motionless as myself!

"Towards it, and now close to it, the boy was running in excited pursuit of the fawn. He stretched out his hands to catch it. It bounded from his eager grasp. Again he reached forward, and again it escaped him. There was another rush forward, and the next instant boy and deer were beneath the tree.

"And now there was no mistaking what I saw.

"The tree was convulsed with motion, leaned forward; swept its thick foliaged boughs to the ground, and enveloped from my sight the pursuer and the pursued; I was within a hundred yards, and the cry of Otona from the midst of the tree came to me in all the clearness of its agony. There was then one stifled, strangling scream, and except for the agitation of the leaves where they had closed upon the boy, there was not a sign of life!

"I called out 'Otona!' No answer came. I tried to call out again, but my utterance was like that of some wild beast smitten at once with sudden terror and its death wound. I stood there, changed from all semblance of a human being. Not all the terrors of earth together could have made me take my eye from the awful plant, or my foot off the ground. I must have stood thus for at least an hour, for the shadows had crept out from the forest half across the glade before that hideous paroxysm of fear left me. My first impulse then was to creep stealthily away lest the tree should perceive me, but my returning reason bade me approach it. The boy might have fallen into the lair of some beast of prey, or perhaps the terrible life in the tree was that of some great serpent among its branches. Preparing to defend myself I approached the silent tree, —the harsh grass crisping beneath my feet with a strange loudness, the cicadas in the forest shrilling till the air seemed throbbing round me with waves of sound. The terrible truth was soon before me in all its awful novelty.

"The vegetable first discovered my presence at about fifty yards distance. I then became aware of a stealthy motion among the thick-lipped leaves, reminding me of some wild beast slowly gathering itself up from long sleep, a vast coil of snakes in restless motion. Have you ever seen bees hanging from a bough—a great cluster of bodies, bee clinging to bee—and by striking the bough, or agitating the air, caused that massed life to begin sulkily to disintegrate, each insect asserting its individual right to move? And do you remember how without one bee leaving the pensile cluster, the whole became gradually instinct with sullen life and horrid with a multitudinous motion?

"I came within twenty yards of it. The tree was quivering through every branch, muttering for blood, and, helpless with rooted feet, yearning with every branch towards me. It was that terror of the deep sea which the men of the northern fiords dread, and which, anchored upon some sunken rock, stretches into vain space its longing arms, pellucid as the sea itself, and as relentless—maimed Polypheme groping for his victims.

"Each separate leaf was agitated and hungry. Like hands they fumbled together, their fleshy palms curling upon themselves and again unfolding, closing on each other and falling apart again, —thick, helpless, fingerless hands (rather lips or tongues than hands) dimpled closely with little cup-like hollows. I approached nearer and nearer, step by step, till I saw that these soft horrors were all of them in motion, opening and closing incessantly.

"I was now within ten yards of the farthest reaching bough. Every part of it was hysterical with excitement. The agitation of its members was awful—sickening yet fascinating. In an ecstasy of eagerness for the food so near them, the leaves turned upon each other. Two meeting would suck together face to face, with a force that compressed their joint thickness to a half, thinning the two leaves into one, now grappling in a volute like a double shell, writhing like some green worm, and at last, faint with the violence of the paroxysm, would slowly separate, falling apart as leeches gorged drop off the limbs. A sticky dew glistened in the dimples, welled over, and trickled down the leaf. The sound of it dripping from leaf to leaf made it seem as if the tree was muttering to itself. The beautiful golden fruit as they swung here and there were clutched now by one leaf and now by another, held for a moment close enfolded from the sight, and then as suddenly released. Here a large leaf, vampire-like, had sucked out the juices of a smaller one. It hung limp and bloodless, like a carcass of which the weasel has tired.

"I watched the terrible struggle till my starting eyes, strained by intense attention, refused their office, and I can hardly say what I saw. But the tree before me seemed to have become a live beast. Above me I felt conscious was a great limb, and each of its thousand clammy hands reached downwards towards me, fumbling. It strained, shivered, rocked, and heaved. It flung itself about in despair. The boughs, tantalized to madness with the presence of flesh, were tossed to this side and to that, in the agony of a frantic desire. The leaves were wrung together as the hands of one driven to madness by sudden misery. I felt the vile dew spurting from the tense veins fall upon me. My clothes began to give out a strange odor. The ground I stood on glistened with animal juices.

"Was I bewildered by terror? Had my senses abandoned me in my need? I know not—but the tree seemed to me to be alive. Leaning over towards me, it seemed to be pulling up its roots from the softened ground, and to be moving towards me. A mountainous monster, with myriad lips, mumbling together for my life, was upon me!

"Like one who desperately defends himself from imminent death, I made an effort for life, and fired my gun at the approaching horror. To my dizzied senses the sound seemed far off, but the shock of the recoil partially recalled me to myself, and starting back I reloaded. The shot had torn their way into the soft body of the great thing. The trunk as it received the wound shuddered, and the whole tree was struck with a sudden quiver. A fruit fell down—slipping from the leaves, now rigid with swollen veins, as from carven foliage. Then I saw a large arm slowly droop, and without a sound it was severed from the juice-fattened bole, and sank down softly, noiselessly, through the glistening leaves. I fired again, and another vile fragment was powerless— dead. At each discharge the terrible vegetable yielded a life. Piecemeal I attacked it, killing here a leaf and there a branch. My fury increased with the slaughter till, when my ammunition was exhausted, the splendid giant was left a wreck as if some hurricane had torn through it. On the ground lay heaped together the fragments, struggling, rising and falling, gasping. Over them drooped in dying languor a few stricken boughs, while upright in the midst stood, dripping at every joint, the glistening trunk.

"My continued firing had brought up one of my men on my mule. He dared not, so he told me, come near me, thinking me mad. I had now drawn my hunting-knife, and with this was fighting—with the leaves. Yes—but each leaf was instinct with a horrid life; and more than once I felt my hand entangled for a moment and seized as if by sharp lips. Ignorant of the presence of my companion I made a rush forward over the fallen foliage, and with a last paroxysm of frenzy drove my knife up to the handle into the soft bole, and, slipping on the fast congealing sap, fell exhausted and unconscious, among the still panting leaves.

"My companions carried me back to the camp, and after vainly searching for Otona awaited my return to consciousness. Two or three hours elapsed before I could speak, and several days before I could approach the terrible thing. My men would not go near it. It was quite dead; for as we came up a great-billed bird with gaudy plumage that had been securely feasting on the decaying fruit, flew up from the wreck. We removed the rotting foliage, and there among the dead leaves still limp with juices, and piled round the roots, we found the ghastly relics of many former meals, and—its last nourishment—the corpse of little Otona. To have re-moved the leaves would have taken too long, so we bur-ied the body as it was with a hundred vampire leaves still clinging to it."

Such, as nearly as I remember it, was my uncle's story of the man-eating tree.

"The Flowering of the Strange Orchid" first appeared in the Pall Mall Budget, *Aug 2, 1984. Apparently having overlooked "The Man-Eating Tree" (1881), Montague Summers listed the Wells story in his* Vampires: Their Kith and Kin, *as the tale that "introduces a botanical vampire."*

THE FLOWERING OF THE STRANGE ORCHID

H. G. WELLS

THE BUYING OF ORCHIDS always has in it a certain speculative flavour. You have before you the brown shrivelled lump of tissue, and for the rest you must trust your judgment, or the auctioneer, or your good-luck, as your taste may incline. The plant may be moribund or dead, or it may be just a respectable purchase, fair value for your money, or perhaps—for the thing has happened again and again—there slowly unfolds before the delighted eyes of the happy purchaser, day after day, some new variety, some novel richness, a strange twist of the labellum, or some subtler coloration or unex-pected mimicry. Pride, beauty, and profit blossom together on one delicate green spike, and it may be, even immortality. For the new miracle of Nature may stand in need of a new specific name, and what so convenient as that of its discoverer? "Johnsmithia"! There have been worse names.

It was perhaps the hope of some such happy discovery that made Winter Wedderburn such a frequent attendant at these sales—that hope, and also, maybe, the fact that he had nothing else of the slightest interest to do in the world. He was a shy, lonely, rather ineffectual man, provided with just enough income to keep off the spur of necessity, and not enough nervous energy to make him seek any exacting employments. He might have collected stamps or coins, or translated Horace, or bound books, or invented new species of diatoms. But, as it happened, he grew orchids, and had one ambitious little hothouse.

"I have a fancy," he said over his coffee, "that something is going to happen to me to-day." He spoke—as he moved and thought—slowly.

"Oh, don't say *that!*" said his housekeeper, who was also his remote cousin. For "something happening" was a euphemism that meant only one thing to her.

"You misunderstand me. I mean nothing unpleasant...though what I do mean I scarcely know."

"To-day," he continued, after a pause, "Peters are going to sell a batch of plants from the Andamans and the Indies. I shall go up and see what they have. It may be I shall buy something good, unawares. That may be it."

He passed his cup for his second cupful of coffee.

"Are these the things collected by that poor young fellow you told me of the other day?" asked his cousin as she filled his cup.

"Yes," he said, and became meditative over a piece of toast.

"Nothing ever does happen to me," he remarked presently, beginning to think aloud. "I wonder why? Things enough happen to other people. There is Harvey. Only the other week, on Monday he picked up sixpence, on Wednesday his chicks all had the staggers, on Friday his cousin came home from Australia, and on Saturday he broke his ankle. What a whirl of excitement—compared to me."

"I think I would rather be without so much excitement," said his housekeeper. "It can't be good for you."

"I suppose it's troublesome. Still—you see, nothing ever happens to me. When I was a little boy I never had accidents. I never fell in love as I grew up. Never married—I wonder how it feels to have something happen to you, something really remarkable."

"That orchid-collector was only thirty-six—twenty years younger than myself—when he died. And he had been married twice, and divorced once; he had had malarial fever four times, and once he broke his thigh. He killed a Malay once, and once he was wounded by a poisoned dart. And in the end he was killed by jungle-leeches. It must have all been very troublesome, but then it must have been very interesting, you know, except, perhaps, the leeches."

"I am sure it was not good for him," said the lady, with conviction.

"Perhaps not." And then Wedderburn looked at his watch. "Twenty-three minutes past eight. I am going up by the quarter to twelve train, so that there is plenty of time. I think I shall wear my alpaca jacket—it is quite warm enough—and my grey felt hat and brown shoes. I suppose—"

He glanced out of the window at the serene sky and sunlit garden, and then nervously at his cousin's face.

"I think you had better take an umbrella if you are going to London," she said, in a voice that admitted of no denial. "There's all between here and the station coming back."

When he returned he was in a state of mild excitement. He had made a purchase. It was rarely that he could make up his mind quickly enough to buy, but this time he had done so.

"There are Vandas," he said, "and a Dendrobe and some Palæonophis." He surveyed his purchases lovingly as he consumed his soup. They were laid out on the spotless tablecloth before him, and he was telling his cousin all about them as he slowly meandered through his dinner. It was his custom to live all his visits to London over again in the evening for her and his own entertainment.

"I knew something would happen to-day. And I have bought all these. Some of them—some of them—I feel sure, do you know, that some of them will be remarkable. I don't know how it is, but I feel just as sure as if someone had told me that some of these will turn out remarkable."

"That one"—he pointed to a shrivelled rhizome—"was not identi-fied. It may be a Palæonophis—or it may not. It may be a new species, or even a new genus. And it was the last that poor Batten ever collected."

"I don't like the look of it," said his housekeeper. "It's such an ugly shape."

"To me it scarcely seems to have a shape."

"I don't like those things that stick out," said his housekeeper.

"It shall be put away in a pot to-morrow."

"It looks," said the housekeeper, "like a spider shamming dead."

Wedderburn smiled and surveyed the root with his head on one side. "It is certainly not a pretty lump of stuff. But you can never judge of these things from their dry appearance. It may turn out to be a very beautiful orchid indeed. How busy I shall be to-morrow! I must see tonight just exactly what to do with these things, and to-morrow I shall set to work.

"They found poor Batten lying dead, or dying, in a mangrove swamp—I forget which," he began again presently, "with one of these very orchids crushed up under his body. He had been unwell for some days with some kind of native fever, and I suppose he fainted.

These mangrove swamps are very unwholesome. Every drop of blood, they say, was taken out of him by the jungle-leeches. It may be that very plant that cost him his life to obtain."

"I think none the better of it for that."

"Men must work though women may weep," said Wedderburn, with profound gravity.

"Fancy dying away from every comfort in a nasty swamp! Fancy being ill of fever with nothing to take but chlorodyne and quinine—if men were left to themselves they would live on chlorodyne and quinine—and no one round you but horrible natives! They say the Andaman islanders are most disgusting wretches—and, anyhow, they can scarcely make good nurses, not having the necessary training. And just for people in England to have orchids!"

"I don't suppose it was comfortable, but some men seem to enjoy that kind of thing," said Wedderburn. "Anyhow, the natives of his party were sufficiently civilized to take care of all his collection until his colleague, who was an ornithologist, came back again from the interior; though they could not tell the species of the orchid and had let it wither. And it makes these things more interesting."

"It makes them disgusting. I should be afraid of some of the malaria clinging to them. And just think, there has been a dead body lying across that ugly thing! I never thought of that before. There! I declare I cannot eat another mouthful of dinner!"

"I will take them off the table if you like, and put them in the windowseat. I can see them just as well there."

The next few days he was indeed singularly busy in his steamy little hot-house, fussing about with charcoal, lumps of teak, moss, and all the other mysteries of the orchid cultivator. He considered he was having a wonderfully eventful time. In the evening he would talk about these new orchids to his friends, and over and over again he reverted to his expectation of something strange.

Several of the Vandas and the Dendrobium died under his care, but presently the strange orchid began to show signs of life. He was delighted and took his housekeeper right away from jam-making to see it at once, directly he made the discovery.

"That is a bud," he said, "and presently there will be a lot of leaves there, and those little things coming out here are aerial rootlets."

"They look to me like little white fingers poking out of the brown," said his housekeeper. "I don't like them."

"Why not?"

"I don't know. They look like fingers trying to get at you. I can't help my likes and dislikes."

"I don't know for certain, but I don't *think* there are any orchids I know that have aerial rootlets quite like that. It may be my fancy, of course. You see they are a little flattened at the ends."

"I don't like 'em," said his housekeeper, suddenly shivering and turning away. "I know it's very silly of me—and I'm very sorry, particularly as you like the thing so much. But I can't help thinking of that corpse."

"But it may not be that particular plant. That was merely a guess of mine."

His housekeeper shrugged her shoulders. "Anyhow I don't like it," she said.

Wedderburn felt a little hurt at her dislike to the plant. But that did not prevent his talking to her about orchids generally, and this orchid in particular, whenever he felt inclined.

"There are such queer things about orchids," he said one day; "such possibilities of surprises. You know, Darwin studied their fertilisation, and showed that the whole structure of an ordinary orchid flower was contrived in order that moths might carry the pollen from plant to plant. Well, it seems that there are lots of orchids known the flower of which cannot possibly be used for fertilisation in that way. Some of the Cypripediums, for instance; there are no insects known that can possibly fertilise them, and some of them have never been found with seed."

"But how do they form new plants?"

"By runners and tubers, and that kind of outgrowth. That is easily explained. The puzzle is, what are the flowers for?

"Very likely," he added, "*my* orchid may be something extraordinary in that way. If so, I shall study it. I have often thought of making researches as Darwin did. But hitherto I have not found the time, or something else has happened to prevent it. The leaves are beginning to unfold now. I do wish you would come and see them!"

But she said that the orchid-house was so hot it gave her a headache. She had seen the plant once again, and the aerial rootlets, which were now some of them more than a foot long, had unfortunately reminded her of tentacles reaching out after something; and they got into her dreams, growing after her with incredible rapidity. So that she had settled to her entire satisfaction that she would not see that plant again, and Wedderburn had to admire its leaves alone. They were of the ordinary broad form, and deep, glossy green, with splashes and dots of deep red towards the base. He knew of no other leaves quite like them. The plant was placed on a low bench near the thermometer, and close by was a simple arrangement by which a tap dripped on the hot-water pipes and kept the air steamy. And he spent his afternoons now with some regularity meditating on the approaching flowering of this strange plant.

And at last the great thing happened. Directly he entered the little glass house he knew that the spike had burst out, although his great *Palæonophis Lowii* hid the corner where his new darling stood. There was a new odour in the air—a rich, intensely sweet scent, that overpowered every other in that crowded, steaming little green-house.

Directly he noticed this he hurried down to the strange orchid. And, *behold!* the trailing green spikes bore now three great splashes of blossom, from which this overpowering sweetness proceeded. He stopped before them in an ecstasy of admiration.

The flowers were white, with streaks of golden orange upon the petals; the heavy labellum was coiled into an intricate projection, and a wonderful bluish purple mingled there with the gold. He could see at once that the genus was altogether a new one. And the insufferable scent! How hot the place was! The blossoms swam before his eyes.

He would see if the temperature was right. He made a step towards the thermometer. Suddenly everything appeared unsteady. The bricks on the floor were dancing up and down. Then the white blossoms, the green leaves behind them, the whole green house, seemed to sweep sideways, and then in a curve upward.

* * * *

At half-past four his cousin made the tea, according to their invariable custom But Wedderburn did not come in for his tea.

"He is worshipping that horrid orchid," she told herself, and waited ten minutes. "His watch must have stopped. I will go and call him."

She went straight to the hothouse, and, opening the door, called his name. There was no reply. She noticed that the air was very close, and loaded with an intense perfume. Then she saw something lying on the bricks between the hot-water pipes.

For a minute, perhaps, she stood motionless.

He was lying, face upward, at the foot of the strange orchid. The tentacle-like aerial rootlets no longer swayed freely in the air, but were crowded together, a tangle of grey ropes, and stretched tight, with their ends closely applied to his chin and neck and hands.

She did not understand. Then she saw from one of the exultant tentacles upon his cheek there trickled a little thread of blood.

With an inarticulate cry she ran towards him, and tried to pull him away from the leech-like suckers. She snapped two of these tentacles, and their sap dripped red.

Then the overpowering scent of the blossom began to make her head reel. How they clung to him! She tore at the tough ropes, and he and the white inflorescence swam about her. She felt she was fainting, knew she must not. She left him and hastily opened the nearest door, and, after she had panted for a moment in the fresh air, she had a brilliant inspiration. She caught up a flower-pot and smashed in the windows at the end of the greenhouse. Then she re-entered. She tugged now with renewed strength at Wedderburn's motionless body, and brought the strange orchid crashing to the floor. It still clung with the grimmest tenacity to its victim. In a frenzy, she lugged it and him into the open air.

Then she thought of tearing through the sucker rootlets one by one, and in another minute she had released him and was dragging him away from the horror.

He was white and bleeding from a dozen circular patches.

The odd-job man was coming up the garden, amazed at the smashing of glass, and saw her emerge, hauling the inanimate body with red-stained hands. For a moment he thought impossible things.

"Bring some water!" she cried, and her voice dispelled his fancies. When, with unnatural alacrity, he returned with the water, he found her weeping with excitement, and with Wedderburn's head upon her knee, wiping the blood from his face.

"What's the matter?" said Wedderburn, opening his eyes feebly, and closing them again at once.

"Go and tell Annie to come out here to me, and then go for Dr. Haddon at once," she said to the odd-job man as soon as he had brought the water, and added, seeing he hesitated: "I will tell you all about it when you come back."

Presently, Wedderburn opened his eyes again, and, seeing that he was troubled by the puzzle of his position, she explained to him: "You fainted in the hothouse."

"And the orchid?"

"I will see to that," she said.

Wedderburn had lost a good deal of blood, but beyond that he had suffered no very great injury. They gave him brandy mixed with some pink extract of meat, and carried him upstairs to bed. His housekeeper told her incredible story in fragments to Dr. Haddon. "Come to the orchid-house and see," she said.

The cold outer air was blowing in through the open door, and the sickly perfume was almost dispelled. Most of the torn aerial rootlets lay already withered amidst a number of dark stains upon the bricks. The stem of the inflorescence was broken by the fall of the plant, and the flowers were growing limp and brown at the edges of the petals. The doctor stooped towards it, then saw that one of the aerial rootlets still stirred feebly, and hesitated.

The next morning the strange orchid still lay there, black now and putrescent. The door banged intermittently in the morning breeze, and all the array of Wedderburn's orchids was shrivelled and prostrate. But Wedderburn himself was bright and garrulous upstairs in the glory of his strange adventure.

"The Story of the Grey House" first appeared in the May 1898 issue of Pearson's Magazine. *It was fifth in a series of a dozen tales featuring Mr. Flaxman Low, the first fictional psychic detective.*

THE STORY OF THE GREY HOUSE

E. & H. HERON

MR. FLAXMAN LOW DECLARES that only on one occasion has he undertaken, unasked, the solving of a psychical mystery. To that case he always refers as the "affair of the Grey House." The house bears a different name in the annals of more than one scientific society, and much controversy has raged over the strange details of a story that seems to open up a new province of fantastic horror. Papers and treatises have been written about it in almost every European language, and many dismaying facts of a somewhat analogous nature have thus been brought to light. There was some hesitation at first about laying this matter—backed as it is by an explanation, which, though terrible, is not altogether unsupported—before the public, but it has finally been decided to incorporate it in the present book.

During the dry summer of 19—, Mr. Low happened to be staying in a lonely village on the coast of Devon. He was deeply immersed in some antiquarian work connected with the old Norse calendars, and therefore limited his acquaintance in the neighbourhood to one individual, a Dr. Fremantle, who, besides being a medical man, was a botanist of some note.

One afternoon, when driving together, Mr. Low and Dr. Fremantle passed through a valley which nestled cup-like in the higher ground a few miles inland. As they passed along a deep, steep lane with overhanging hedges they caught a glimpse, through a break in the leaves, of a grey gable visible between the horizontal branches of a cedar.

Flaxman Low pointed it out to his companion.

"That's young Montesson's house," answered Fremantle, "and it bears a very sinister reputation. Nothing in your line, though," with a smile. "Indeed, no ghost would lend the same hideous associations to the place it now possesses as the result of a succession of mysterious murders that have occurred there."

"The grounds seem neglected. I don't remember to have seen such rank growth anywhere."

"Certainly not inside the British Isles," returned Fremantle.

"The estate is left to take care of itself, partly because Montesson won't live there, partly because it is impossible to find labourers to work near the house. Our warm, damp climate and this sheltered position give rise to extraordinary luxuriance of growth. A stream runs along the bottom, and I expect all the low-lying land, where you see that belt of yellow African grass, is little better than a morass now."

Fremantle drew up as they gained the top of the slope. From there they could overlook the tangle of vegetation, dimmed by a rising mist, which surrounded and almost hid the roof of the Grey House.

"Yes," said Freemantle, in answer to an observation of Mr. Low, "Montesson's guardian, who lived here and looked after the property for him, turned the place into a subtropical garden. It used to be one of my chief pleasures to wander about here, but since my marriage my wife objects to my doing so, on account of the tales she has heard."

"What is the danger?"

"Death!" replied Fremantle shortly.

"What form of death? Malaria?"

"No disease at all, my dear fellow. The persons who die at the Grey House are hanged by the neck until they are dead!"

"Hanged?" repeated Flaxman Low in surprise.

"Yes, hanged. Not only strangled but suspended, as the marks on the necks show. If there were any hint of a ghost in it you might investigate—Montesson would be only too grateful if you could fathom the mystery."

"Tell me something more definite."

"I'll tell you what has happened within my own knowledge. Montesson's father died some fifteen years ago and left him to the guardianship of a cousin named Lampurt, who, as I told you, was a horticulturist, and planted the place with a wonderful variety of foreign shrubs and flowers. Lampurt had a bad name in the country, and his appearance was certainly against him—a squint-eyed, pig-faced fellow, who sidled along like a crab, and could not look you in the face. He died first."

"Was he hanged? Or did he hang himself?"

"Neither, in this case. He dropped in a kind of fit, right up in front of the house, while he was engaged in planting some new acquisition. Had it not been for the evidence of the persons who were present at the time, I should have said his death resulted from some tremendous mental shock. But the gardener and his relation, Mrs. Montesson, agreed in saying that he was not exerting himself unduly, and that he had had no disturbing news. He was a healthy man and I could see no sufficient reason for his death. He was simply gardening, and had apparently pricked himself with a nail, for he had a spot of blood upon his forefinger.

"After that all went well for a couple of years, when, during the summer holidays, the trouble began. Montesson must have been about sixteen at the time, and had a tutor with him. His mother and sister—a pretty girl rather older than himself—were also here. One morning the girl was found lying on the gravel under her window, quite dead. I was sent for, and, upon examination, discovered the extraordinary fact that she had been hanged!"

"Murder?"

"Of course, though we could find no trace of the murderer. The girl had been taken from her bedroom and hanged. Then the rope was removed and she was thrown in a heap under her window. The crime caused a tremendous sensation in the neighbourhood, and the police were busy for a long time, but nothing came of their inquiries.

"About a fortnight later, Platt, the tutor, sat up smoking at the open study window. In the morning he was found lying out over the sill. There could be no mistake as to how he met his death, for in addition to the deep line round his throat, his neck was broken as neatly as they could have done it at Newgate! As in the other case, there was nothing to show how he came by his death, no rope, no trace of footsteps or any struggle to lead one to suspect the presence of another person or persons. Yet from the facts it could not have been suicide."

"I see you had some suspicion of your own," said Flaxman Low.

"Well, yes, I had. But time has passed, and I now think I must have been mistaken. I must explain that the branches of the cedar you saw jut to within a few feet of the windows of the rooms occupied by Miss

Montesson and Platt respectively, at the time of death. I told you there were no traces of anyone having approached the house. It therefore struck me that some active person might have leaped from the cedar into the open windows and escaped in the same way, for the windows open vertically, and when both leaves are thrown back, there is a large aperture. But the murders were so purposeless and disconnected that they suggested irresponsible agency. I recollected Poe's story of the Rue Morgue, where, you remember, the crimes were committed by an ourang-outang. It seemed to me possible that Lampurt, who was of a morose and strange temper, might, among other things, have secretly imported an ape and turned it loose in the woods. I had a thorough search made in the park and grounds, but we found nothing, and I have long ago abandoned the theory."

Low thought silently over the story for some time, then he asked for the dates of the three deaths. Fremantle answered categorically, and it appeared that all had taken place about the same season of the year—during summer, in fact. Upon this Mr. Low made an offer to investigate the affair on psychical lines, if Montesson made no objection. In answer to this message Montesson took the next train down to Devon, and begged to be allowed to accompany Mr. Low in his inquiries.

Flaxman Low quickly saw that Montesson might prove a very useful companion. He was a blond, heavily-built man, and plainly possessed of a strong will and temper. Low put aside his books and went off at once with Montesson to have a closer look at the Grey House while the daylight lasted.

It is difficult to give any adequate impression of the teeming exuberance of wild and tangled growth through which they had to cut their way. Young, lush, sappy leafage overlay and half disguised the dank rottenness of the older vegetation beneath. After wading more than breast-high through the malted reeds, below which the spreading stream was fast reducing the land to a swamp, they emerged into a fairly open space that had once been the lawn round the house.

Here brambled and lusty weeds now grew abundantly under the untended trees. Curious shrubs and plants flourished here and there. As they came up, a stoat sneaked away by a narrow footpath, nettle-grown and caked with damp, which led past blackened bushes round the house. Otherwise the place was deserted; not a leaf seemed to move in the windless heat of the afternoon. The squat, grey face of the house was scarred across by a dark-leaved creeper, hung with orchid-like blossoms, a little to the left of which Low noticed the cedar mentioned by Dr. Fremantle.

Low drew up at the weed-twisted, sunken little gate that gave upon the lawns and spoke for the first time.

"Tell me about it," and he nodded towards the house.

Montesson repeated the story already told, but added further details. "From here," went on Montesson, "you can see the exact spot where all these things took place. The upper of these two windows surrounded by the creeper and under the shadow of the cedar, belonged to my sister's room; the lower is that of the study where Platt died. The gravel path below ran the whole length of the house, but it is now over-grown.... Has Fremantle told you of Lawrence?"

Low shook his head.

"I hate the very sight of the place!" said Montesson hoarsely; "the mystery and the horror of it all seem in my blood. I can't forget!--my mother left on the day of Platt's death, and has never been here since. But when I came of age I resolved to make another attempt to live here, meaning to sift the past if I got the chance of doing so. I had the grounds cleared about the house, and after leaving Oxford, came down with a man of my own year, called Lawrence. We spent the Easter vacation here reading, and all went right enough. Meanwhile, I had the house examined, thinking there might be a secret entrance or room, but nothing of the kind exists. This house is not haunted. Nothing has ever been seen or heard of a supernatural character— nothing but the same, awful repetition of blind murder!"

After a few seconds he resumed.

"During the following summer Lawrence came down with me again. One hot evening we were smoking as we walked up and down the gravel under the windows. It was bright moonlight, and I remember the heavy scent of those red flowers—" Montesson glanced round him strangely.

"I went in to fetch a cigar. It took me some minutes to find the box I wanted, and to light the cigar. When I came out, Lawrence lay crumpled up as if he had fallen from a height, and he was dead. Round his neck was the same bluish line I had seen in the two other cases. You can understand what it was to leave the man not five minutes before, in health and strength, and to come back to find him, dead—hanged—to judge from appearances! But, as usual, no trace of rope or struggle or murderer!"

After some further talk, Mr. Low proposed to go into the house. It had evidently been deserted in haste. In the room once occupied by Miss Montesson, her girlish treasures still lay about, dusty, moth-eaten, and discoloured. Montesson paused on the threshold.

"Poor little Fan! It's just as she left it!" he said hurriedly.

The cedar outside threw a gloomy shade into the room, and the fantastic red blossoms drooped motionless in the stagnant air.

"Was the window open when your sister was found?" inquired Low, after he had examined the room.

"Yes, it was hot weather—early in August. This room has not been occupied since. After Platt's affair, I have always avoided this side of the house, so that it was only by chance Lawrence and I came round to this part of the lawn to smoke."

"Then we may suppose that the danger, whatever it is, exists on this side of the house only?"

"So it seems," replied Montesson.

"Your sister was last seen alive in this room? Platt in the room directly below?—and your friend—what of him?"

"Lawrence was lying on the gravel path just under the study window. All of them have died under the shadow of the cedar. Did Fremantle give you his idea? Poor Lawrence's death disposed of that theory. No big ape could live in England all those five years in the open, and in any case it must have been seen sometime in the interval."

"I think so," replied Low, abstractedly. "Now as to what we must do to try and get at the meaning of all this. Do you feel equal, considering all you have gone through in this house, do you feel equal to remaining here with me for a night or two?"

Montesson again glanced over his shoulder nervously.

"Yes," he said. "I know my nerves are not as stiff and steady as they should be, but I'll stand by you— especially as you would not find another man about here willing to run the risk. You see it is not a ghost or any fanciful trouble, it means a real danger. Think over it, Mr. Low, before you undertake so hazardous an attempt."

Low looked into the blue eyes Montesson had fixed upon him. They were weary, anxious eyes, and, taken in combination with his compressed lips and square chin, told Low of the struggle this man constantly endured between his shaken nervous system and the strong will that mastered it.

"If you'll stand by me, I'll try to get to the bottom of it," said Low.

"I wonder if 1 should allow you to risk your life in this way?" returned Montesson, passing his hand over his prematurely-lined forehead.

"Why not? Besides, it is my own wish. As for risking our lives—it is for the good of mankind."

"I can't say I see it in that light." said Montesson in surprise.

"If we lose our lives it will be in the effort to make another spot of earth clean and wholesome and safe for men to live on. Our duty to the public requires us to run a murderer to earth. Here we have a murderous power of some subtle kind; is it not quite as much our duty to destroy it if we can, even at risk to ourselves?"

The result of this conversation was an arrangement to pass the night at the Grey House. About ten o'clock they set out, intending to follow the path they had more or less successfully cleared for themselves in the afternoon. By Flaxman Low's advice, Montesson carried a long knife. The night was unusually hot and still, and lit only by a thin moon as they made their way along, stumbling over matted weeds and roots and literally feeling for the path, until they came to the little gate by the lawn. There they stopped a moment to look at the house, standing out among its strange sea of overgrowth, the dim moon low on the horizon, glinting palely upon the windows and over the deserted countryside. As they waited, a night-bird hooted and flapped its way across the open.

At any moment they might be at hand-grips with the mysterious power of death which haunted the place. The warm lush-scented air and the sinister shadows seemed charged with some ominous influence. As they drew near the house Low perceived a sweet, heavy odour.

"What is it?" he asked.

"It comes from those scarlet flowers, at night. It's unbearable! Lampurt imported the thing," replied Montesson irritably.

"Which room will you spend the night in?" asked Low as they gained the hall.

Montesson hesitated. "Have you ever heard the expression 'grey with fear'?" he said, laughing in the dark; "I'm that!"

Low did not like the laugh; it was only one remove, and that a very little one, from hysteria.

"We won't find out much unless we each remain alone and with open windows as they did," said Low.

Montesson shook himself.

"No, I suppose not. They were each alone when— good-night, I'll call if anything happens, and you must do the same for me. For Heaven's sake, don't go to sleep!"

"And remember," added Low, "with your knife to cut at anything that touches you." Then he stood at the study door and listened to Montesson's heavy steps as they passed up the stairs, for he had elected to pass the night in his sister's room. Low heard him walk across the floor and throw wide the window.

When Mr. Low turned into the study and tried to open the window there, he found it impossible to do so; the creeper outside had fastened upon the woodwork, binding the sashes together. There was but one thing left for him to do; he must go outside and stand where Lawrence had stood on the fatal night. He let himself out softly and went round to the south side of the house.

There he paced up and down in the shadows for perhaps an hour.

In the deceptive, iridescent moonlight, a pallid head seemed to wag at him from the gloom below the cedar, but, moving towards it, he grasped only the yellow bunched blossoms of a giant ragwort. Then he stood still and looked up into the branches above; the gnarled black branches with their fringes of black sticky leaves. Fremantle's theory of the ape passing stealthily among them to spring upon his victim found a sudden horror of possibility in Low's mind. He imagined the girl awaking in the brute's cruel hands....

Out upon the quiet brooding of the night broke a scream—or rather a roar, a harsh, jagged, pulsating roar, that ceased as abruptly as it had begun.

Without a moment's consideration, Mr. Low seized the branch nearest to him and, swinging himself up into the tree, he climbed with a frantic effort towards the window of Montesson's room, from which he was almost sure the sound had come. Being an unusually active and athletic man he leaped from the branch towards the open window, and fell headlong in upon the floor. As he did so, something seemed to pass him, something swift and sinuous that might have been a snake, and disappear out of the window!

Remembering a candle on the toilet table, he lit it when he regained his feet and looked about him.

Montesson lay on the floor "crumpled up" as he had himself described Lawrence's position. Low recalled this with misgiving, as he hurried to his side. A dark smear like blood was on Montesson's cheek, but though unconscious, he was still alive. Low lifted him on to the bed and did what he could to rouse him, but without success. He lay rigid, breathing the slow, almost imperceptible, respiration of deep stupor.

Low was about to go to the window, when the candle suddenly went out, and he was left in the increasing darkness, to all intents alone, to face an unknown though tangible assailant.

Silence had again fallen upon the house—that is, the silence of night, and woodlands, and many-folded leafage, and the things that go by night. He stood by the window and listened. His senses were acute and throbbing; he felt as if he could hear for miles. The scent of the scarlet blossoms rose like deadening fumes into his brain, and he drew away from the window; and, feeling strangely spent, threw himself upon a couch. Then he drew out the knife at his belt, and strung himself up to watchfulness with an effort.

He knew that the attack he had to expect would be likely to come from the direction of the window. He saw the faint, swimming moonlight that fell through the leaves and tendrils of the creeper fade slowly away. Probably clouds were coming up over the sky, for the steamy heat was even more oppressive.

The low window-sill was scarcely more than a foot above the floor, and presently he fancied something was moving along the carpet among the entangling shadows of the leaves, but the darkness was now intensified, and he could not be sure. Montesson's breathing had become quieter. It was the dead hour of the night; hardly a sound was to be heard.

Suddenly Low felt a soft touch upon his knee. His whole consciousness had been so absorbed in the act of listening that this unexpected appeal to another sense startled him. Here and there, rapid, soft, and light, the touches passed over his body. It might have been some animal nosing about him in the dark. Then a smooth, told touch fell upon his cheek.

Low sprang up, and slashed about him in the darkness with his knife.

In that instant the thing closed with him—a flexuous, snaky thing that flung its coils about his limbs and body in one swift spring like a curling whiplash!

Flaxman Low was all but helpless in the winding grasp of what?--the tentacles of some strange creature? Or was it some great snake, this sentient thing that was feeling for his throat? There was not an instant to lose. The knife was pressed against his body; with a violent effort he drew it sharply, edge outwards, against the tightening coils. A spurt of clammy fluid fell upon his hand, and the thing loosed and fell away from him into the stifling gloom.

In the morning Montesson came to himself in one of the lower rooms at the other side of the house. Fremantle was beside him.

"What's the matter?" he asked. "Ah, I remember now. There's Low. It has beaten us again, Fremantle! It is hopeless. I don't know what happened—I was not asleep, when I found myself seized, lifted up, drawn towards the window, and strangled by loving ropes. Look at Low!" he went on harshly, raising himself. "Why, man, you're all over blood!"

Flaxman Low glanced down at his hands.

"Looks like it," he said.

"It has beaten even you, Low!" went on Montesson. "There is something much more terrible and tangible than a ghost in this cursed house! See here!"

He pulled down his collar. A faint bluish circle with suffused dots was drawn round his throat.

"It is some deadly species of snake," exclaimed Fremantle.

Low sat down thoughtfully, astride a chair. "I'm sorry to disagree with both of you. But I am inclined to think it is not a snake, and on the other hand I fancy it has a great deal to do with what we may roughly call a ghost. The whole evidence points in only one direction."

"You mustn't let your prejudice in favour of psychical problems run away with your reason," said Fremantle drily. "Has a ghost actual, palpable power?— to go further, has it blood?"

Montesson, who had been looking at his neck in the glass, turned quickly. "It's some horrible thing in nature! Something between a snake and an octopus! What do you say to it, Low?"

Low looked up gravely.

"In spite of Fremantle's objections the steps from the beginning to end are very clear."

Fremantle and Montesson exchanged a glance of incredulity.

"My dear fellow, much learning has warped your mind," said Fremantle with an embarrassed laugh.

"First of all," continued Low, "we know where all the deaths have occurred."

"To speak precisely, they have all occurred in different places," interposed Fremantle.

"True; but within a strictly limited area. The slight differences have been of material help to me. In all cases they have occurred in the vicinity of one thing."

"The cedar!" cried Montesson, with some excitement.

"That was my first idea—now I refer to the wall. Will you tell me the probable weight of Lawrence and Platt at the date of death?"

"Platt was a small man—perhaps under nine stone. Lawrence, though much taller, was thin, and could not have weighed more than eleven. As for poor little Fan, she was only a slip of a girl."

"Three people have been killed—one has escaped. In what way do you differ from the others, Montesson?" asked Low.

"If you mean I'm heavier, I certainly am. I scale something like fifteen. But what has that to do with it?"

"Everything. The coils have evidently not sufficient compressive power to destroy life by strangulation simply—there must be suspension as well. You were simply too heavy for them to tackle."

"Coils of what?"

"Of this." Low held up a tapering, reddish-brown tendon or line, which had red curved triangular teeth set on it at intervals.

The two other men stared at this object, and then Montesson burst out. "The creeper on the wall!" he said, in a tone of disappointment. "It couldn't be! Besides, has a plant blood?"

"Let us go and look at it," said Low. "This creeper has never been cut because it withers away to the ground every winter and grows again in the spring. Look here!" He took out his knife and cut a leathery shoot. A crimson stain spurted out on his cuff. "The only person, as far as I can gather, who cut this plant was Mr. Lampurt in nailing it to the wall. He died of shock when he saw the red stain on his finger, as he knew something of its deadly properties. But though stupefying—as your condition last night proved, Montesson—they are not fatal. Even to stupefy they must get into the blood. Now the deaths have all occurred within reach of the tendrils of this plant. And all have happened at the same season of the year, that is to say, at the time when it attains its full annual strength and growth. Another point in favour of Montesson's escape was the dryness of the season. The growth is not quite so good as usual this summer, is it?"

"No, the tendrils are thinner—a good deal thinner and smaller."

"Just so. Therefore your weight saved you, though you were stupefied by the punctures of the thorns. I feared that, and warned you to use your knife."

"But the brain of the thing?" cried Fremantle. "Why, man, has a plant will and knowledge and malevolence?"

"Not of itself, as I believe," answered Low. "Perhaps you will prefer to attribute much to the long arm of coincidence, but the explanation I can offer is one that has long been held by occultists in other countries. Pythagoras and others have taught that the forms of incarnation change as the soul raises or debases itself during each spell of life. Connect with this the belief of the Brahmins, and, I may add, of various African tribes, that an earth-bound spirit, at the moment of a premature or sudden death, may pass into plants or trees of certain species, by virtue of an inherent attraction possessed by these plants for such entities. To go further, it is said that these degraded souls have intervals during which they have power of voluntary action to do good or evil, and such action has influence on their future incarnations."

"What do you mean? What do you intend us to believe?" Montesson said, and stopped.

"It is hard to put it into words in these later days of unbelief," said Low, "but the evidence goes to show that a man—presumably not a good man—dies a sudden death near this plant, even inoculated with its sap. Fremantle knows this plant to be a Malayan creeper, belonging to a family that possess strange power and properties. I may recall the old story of the upas tree, and more lately still the murder tree discovered near Kolwe, in East Africa, by Herr Boltze. There are also other instances."

"It is incredible!" said Fremantle almost angrily.

"I don't ask you to believe it," said Flaxman Low quietly, "I only tell you such beliefs exist. Montesson can do something towards proving my theory. Let him have the plant destroyed, and judge by the results."

The tendril of the creeper severed by Mr. Low in his struggle was presented by him to the authorities at Kew.

Mr. Montesson has acted upon Mr. Flaxman Low's suggestions. The Grey House is now occupied and safe, and it is a strange fact that no plant, not even the hardy ivy, will live where the red-blossomed creeper once grew.

"The Purple Terror" first appeared in the September 1899 issue of The Strand. *The story takes place shortly after the Spanish-American War (April 25-August 12, 1898). As a result of the war, the United States gained control over Spain's colonial territories in the Caribbean: Puerto Rico became a Commonwealth of the U.S. in 1898, and in 1902, Cuba was declared independent. Although the U.S. lost 279 men in combat, over 5000 more perished from disease.*

THE PURPLE TERROR

FRED M. WHITE

I

LIEUTENANT WILL SCARLETT'S instructions were devoid of problems, physical or otherwise. To convey a letter from Captain Driver of the *Yankee Doodle*, in Porto Rico Bay, to Admiral Lake on the other side of the isthmus, was an apparently simple matter.

"All you have to do," the captain remarked, "is to take three or four men with you in case of accidents, cross the isthmus on foot, and simply give this letter into the hands of Admiral Lake. By so doing we shall save at least four days, and the aborigines are presumedly friendly."

The aborigines aforesaid were Cuban insurgents. Little or no strife had taken place along the neck lying between Porto Rico and the north bay where Lake's flagship lay, though the belt was known to be given over to the disaffected Cubans.

"It is a matter of fifty miles through practically unexplored country," Scarlett replied; "and there's a good deal of the family quarrel in this business, sir. If the Spaniards hate us, the Cubans are not exactly enamoured of our flag."

Captain Driver roundly denounced the whole pack of them.

"Treacherous thieves to a man," he said. "I don't suppose your progress will have any brass bands and floral arches to it. And they tell me the forest is pretty thick. But you'll get there all the same. There is the letter, and you can start as soon as you like."

"I may pick my own men, sir?"

"My dear fellow, take whom you please. Take the mastiff, if you like."

"I'd like the mastiff," Scarlett replied; "as he is practically my own, I thought you would not object."

Will Scarlett began to glow as the prospect of adventure stimulated his imagination. He was rather a good specimen of West Point naval dandyism. He had brains at the back of his smartness, and his geological and botanical knowledge were going to prove of considerable service to a grateful country when said grateful country should have passed beyond the rudimentary stages of colonization. And there was some disposition to envy Scarlett on the part of others floating for the past month on the liquid prison of the sapphire sea.

A warrant officer, Tarrer by name, *plus* two A.B.'s of thews and sinews, to say nothing of the dog, completed the exploring party. By the time that the sun kissed the tip of the feathery hills they had covered some six miles of their journey. From the first Scarlett had been struck by the absolute absence of the desolation and horror of civil strife. Evidently the fiery cross had not been carried here; huts and houses were intact; the villagers stood under sloping eaves, and regarded the Americans with a certain sullen curiosity.

"We'd better stop for the night here," said Scarlett.

They had come at length to a village that boasted some pretensions. An adobe chapel at one end of the straggling street was faced by a wine-house at the other.

A padre, with hands folded over a bulbous, greasy gabardine, bowed gravely to Scarlett's salutation. The latter had what Tarrer called "considerable Spanish."

"We seek quarters for the night," said Scarlett. "Of course, we are prepared to pay for them."

The sleepy padre nodded towards the wine-house.

"You will find fair accommodations there," he said. "We are friends of the Americanos."

Scarlett doubted the fact, and passed on with florid thanks. So far, little signs of friendliness had been encountered on the march. Coldness, suspicion, a suggestion of fear, but no friendliness to be embarrassing.

The keeper of the wine-shop had his doubts. He feared his poor accommodation for guests so distinguished. A score or more of picturesque, cut-throat-looking rascals with cigarettes in their mouths lounged sullenly in the bar. The display of a brace of gold dollars enlarged mine host's opinion of his household capacity.

"I will do my best, señors," he said. "Come this way."

So it came to pass that an hour after twilight Tarrer and Scarlett were seated in the open amongst the oleanders and the trailing gleam of the fire-flies, discussing cigars of average merit and a native wine that was not without virtues. The long bar of the wine-house was brilliantly illuminated; from within came shouts of laughter mingled with the ting, tang of the guitar and the rollicking clack of the castanets.

"They seem to be happy in there," Tarrer remarked. "It isn't all daggers and ball in this distressful country."

A certain curiosity came over Scarlett.

"It is the duty of a good officer," he said, "to lose no opportunity of acquiring useful information. Let us join the giddy throng, Tarrer."

Tarrer expressed himself with enthusiasm in favour of any amusement that might be going. A month's idleness on shipboard increases the appetite for that kind of thing wonderfully. The long bar was comfortable, and filled with Cubans who took absolutely no notice of the intruders. Their eyes were turned towards a rude stage at the far end of the bar, whereon a girl was gyrating in a dance with a celerity and grace that caused the wreath of flowers around her shoulders to resemble a trembling zone of purple flame.

"A wonderfully pretty girl and a wonderfully pretty dance," Scarlett murmured, when the motions ceased and the girl leapt gracefully to the ground. "Largesse, I expect. I thought so. Well, I'm good for a quarter."

The girl came forward, extending a shell prettily. She curtsied before Scarlett and fixed her dark, liquid eyes on his. As he smiled and dropped his quarter-dollar into the shell a coquettish gleam came into the velvety eyes. An ominous growl came from the lips of a bearded ruffian close by.

"Othello's jealous," said Tarrer. "Look at his face."

"I am better employed," Scarlett laughed. "That was a graceful dance, pretty one. I hope you are going to give us another one presently—"

Scarlett paused suddenly. His eyes had fallen on the purple band of flowers the girl had twined round her shoulder. Scarlett was an enthusiastic botanist; he knew most of the gems in Flora's crown, but he had never looked upon such a vivid wealth of blossom before.

The flowers were orchids, and orchids of a kind unknown to collectors anywhere. On this point Scarlett felt certain. And yet this part of the world was by no means a difficult one to explore in comparison with New Guinea and Sumatra, where the rarer varieties had their homes.

The blooms were immensely large, far larger than any flower of the kind known to Europe or America, of a deep pure purple, with a blood-red centre. As Scarlett gazed upon them he noticed a certain cruel expression on the flower. Most orchids have a kind of face of their own; the purple blooms had a positive expression of ferocity and cunning. They exhumed, too, a queer, sickly fragrance. Scarlett had smelt something like it before, after the Battle of Manila. The perfume was the perfume of a corpse.

"And yet they are magnificent flowers," said Scarlett. "Won't you tell me where you got them from, pretty one?"

The girl was evidently flattered by the attention bestowed upon her by the smart young American. The bearded Othello alluded to edged up to her side.

"The señor had best leave the girl alone," he said, insolently.

Scarlett's fist clenched as he measured the Cuban with his eyes. The Admiral's letter crackled in his breast-pocket, and discretion got the best of valour.

"You are paying yourself a poor compliment, my good fellow," he said, "though I certainly admire your good taste. Those flowers interested me."

The man appeared to be mollified. His features corrugated in a smile.

"The señor would like some of those blooms?" he asked. "It was I who procured them for little Zara here. I can show you where they grow."

Every eye in the room was turned in Scarlett's direction. It seemed to him that a kind of diabolical malice glistened on every dark face there, save that of the girl, whose features paled under her healthy tan.

"If the señor is wise," she began, "he will not—"

"Listen to the tales of a silly girl," Othello put in menacingly. He grasped the girl by the arm, and she winced in positive pain. "Pshaw, there is no harm where the flowers grow, if one is only careful. I will take you there, and I will be your guide to Port Anna, where you are going, for a gold dollar."

All Scarlett's scientific enthusiasm was aroused. It is not given to every man to present a new orchid to the horticultural world. And this one would dwarf the finest plant hitherto discovered.

"Done with you," he said; "we start at daybreak. I shall look to you to be ready. Your name is Tito? Well, good-night, Tito."

As Scarlett and Tarrer withdrew the girl suddenly darted forward. A wild word or two fluttered from her lips. Then there was a sound as of a blow, followed by a little stifled cry of pain.

"No, no," Tarrer urged, as Scarlett half turned. "Better not. They are ten to one, and they are no friends of ours. It never pays to interfere in these family quarrels. I daresay, if you interfered, the girl would be just as ready to knife you as her jealous lover."

"But a blow like that, Tarrer!"

"It's a pity, but I don't see how we can help it. Your business is the quick dispatch of the Admiral's letter, not the squiring of dames."

Scarlett owned with a sigh that Tarrer was right.

II

It was quite a different Tito who presented himself at daybreak the following morning. His insolent manner had disappeared. He was cheerful, alert, and he had a manner full of the most winning politeness.

"You quite understand what we want," Scarlett said. "My desire is to reach Port Anna as soon as possible. You know the way?"

"Every inch of it, señor. I have made the journey scores of times. And I shall have the felicity of getting you there early on the third day from now."

"Is it so far as that?"

"The distance is not great, señor. It is the passage through the woods. There are parts where no white man has been before."

"And you will not forget the purple orchids?"

A queer gleam trembled like summer lightning in Tito's eyes. The next instant it had gone. A time was to come when Scarlett was to recall that look, but for the moment it was allowed to pass.

"The señor shall see the purple orchid," he said; "thousands of them. They have a bad name amongst our people, but that is all nonsense. They grow in the high trees, and their blossoms cling to long, green tendrils. These tendrils are poisonous to the flesh, and great care should be taken in handling them. And the flowers are quite harmless, though we call them the devil's poppies."

To all of this Scarlett listened eagerly. He was all-impatient to see and handle the mysterious flower for himself. The whole excursion was going to prove a wonderful piece of luck. At the same time he had to curb his impatience. There would be no chance of seeing the purple orchid to-day.

For hours they fought their way along through the dense tangle. A heat seemed to lie over all the land like a curse—a blistering, sweltering, moist heat with no puff of wind to temper its breathlessness. By the time that the sun was sliding down, most of the party had had enough of it.

They passed out of the underwood at length, and, striking upwards, approached a clump of huge forest trees on the brow of a ridge. All kinds of parasites hung from the branches; there were ropes and bands of green, and high up a fringe of purple glory that caused Scarlett's pulses to leap a little faster.

"Surely that is the purple orchid?" he cried.

Tito shrugged his shoulders contemptuously.

"A mere straggler or two," he said, "and out of reach in any case. The señor will have all he wants and more to-morrow."

"But it seems to me," said Scarlett, "that I could—"

Then he paused. The sun like a great glowing shield was shining full behind the tree with its crown of purple, and showing up every green rope and thread clinging to the branches with the clearness of liquid crystal. Scarlett saw a network of green cords like a huge spider's web, and in the centre of it was not a fly, but a human skeleton!

The arms and legs were stretched apart as if the victim had been crucified. The wrists and ankles were bound in the cruel web. Fragments of tattered clothing fluttered in the faint breath of the evening breeze.

"Horrible," Scarlett cried, "absolutely horrible!"

"You may well say that," Tarrer exclaimed, with a shudder. "Like the fly in the amber or the apple in the dumpling, the mystery is how he got there."

"Perhaps Tito can explain the mystery," Scarlett suggested.

Tito appeared to be uneasy and disturbed. He looked furtively from one to the other of his employers as a culprit might who feels he has been found out. But his courage returned as he noted the absence of suspicion in the faces turned upon him.

"I can explain," he exclaimed, with teeth that chattered from some unknown terror or guilt. "It is not the first time that I have seen the skeleton. Some plant-hunter doubtless who came here alone. He climbed into the tree without a knife, and those green ropes got twisted round his limbs, as a swimmer gets entangled in the weeds. The more he struggled, the more the cords bound him. He would call in vain for anyone to assist him here. And so he must have died."

The explanation was a plausible one, but by no means detracted from the horror of the discovery. For some time the party pushed their way on in the twilight, till the darkness descended suddenly like a curtain.

"We will camp here," Tito said; "it is high, dry ground, and we have this belt of trees above us. There is no better place than this for miles around. In the valley the miasma is dangerous."

As Tito spoke he struck a match, and soon a torch flamed up. The little party were on a small plateau, fringed by trees. The ground was dry and hard, and, as Scarlett and his party saw to their astonishment, littered with bones. There were skulls of animals and skulls of human beings, the skeletons of birds, the frames of beasts both great and small. It was a weird, shuddering sight.

"We can't possibly stay here," Scarlett exclaimed.

Tito shrugged his shoulders.

"There is nowhere else," he replied. "Down in the valley there are many dangers. Further in the woods are the snakes and jaguars. Bones are nothing. Peuf, they can be easily cleared away."

They had to be cleared away, and there was an end of the matter. For the most part the skeletons were white and dry as air and sun could make them. Over the dry, calcined mass the huge fringe of trees nodded mournfully. With the rest, Scarlett was busy scattering the mocking frames aside. A perfect human skeleton lay at his feet. On one finger something glittered—a signet ring. As Scarlett took it in his hand he started.

"I know this ring!" he exclaimed; "it belonged to Pierre Anton, perhaps the most skilled and intrepid plant-hunter the *Jardin des Plantes* ever employed. The poor fellow was by way of being a friend of mine. He met the fate that he always anticipated."

"There must have been a rare holocaust here," said Tarrer.

"It beats me," Scarlett responded. By this time a large circle had been shifted clear of human and other remains. By the light of the fire loathsome insects could be seen scudding and straddling away. "It beats me entirely. Tito, can you offer any explanation? If the bones were all human I could get some grip of the problem. But when one comes to birds and animals as well! Do you see that the skeletons lie in a perfect circle, starting from the centre of the clump of trees above us? What does it mean?"

Tito professed utter ignorance of the subject. Some years before a small tribe of natives invaded the peninsula for religious rites. They came from a long way off in canoes, and wild stories were told concerning them. They burnt sacrifices, no doubt.

Scarlett turned his back contemptuously on this transparent tale. His curiosity was aroused. There must be some explanation, for Pierre Anton had been seen of men within the last ten years.

"There's something uncanny about this," he said to Tarrer. "I mean to get to the bottom of it, or know why."

"As for me," said Tarrer, with a cavernous yawn, "I have but one ambition, and that is my supper, followed by my bed."

III

Scarlett lay in the light of the fire looking about him. He felt restless and uneasy, though he would have found it difficult to explain the reason. For one thing, the air trembled to strange noises. There seemed to be something moving, writhing in the forest trees above his head. More than once it seemed to his distorted fancy that he could see a squirming knot of green snakes in motion.

Outside the circle, in a grotto of bones, Tito lay sleeping. A few moments before his dark, sleek head had been furtively raised, and his eyes seemed to gleam in the flickering firelight with malignant cunning. As he met Scarlett's glance he gave a deprecatory gesture and subsided.

"What the deuce does it all mean?" Scarlett muttered. "I feel certain yonder rascal is up to some mischief. Jealous still because I paid his girl a little attention. But he can't do us any real harm. Quiet, there!"

The big mastiff growled and then whined uneasily. Even the dog seemed to be conscious of some unseen danger. He lay down again, cowed by the stern command, but he still whimpered in his dreams.

"I fancy I'll keep awake for a spell," Scarlett told himself.

For a time he did so. Presently he began to slide away into the land of poppies. He was walking amongst a garden of bones which bore masses of purple blossoms. Then Pierre Anton came on the scene, pale and resolute as Scarlett had always known him; then the big mastiff seemed in some way to be mixed up with the phantasm of the dream, barking as if in pain, and Scarlett came to his senses.

He was breathing short, a beady perspiration stood on his forehead, his heart hammered in quick thuds— all the horrors of nightmare were still upon him. In a vague way as yet he heard the mastiff howl, a real howl of real terror, and Scarlett knew that he was awake.

Then a strange thing happened. In the none too certain light of the fire, Scarlett saw the mastiff snatched up by some invisible hand, carried far on high towards the trees, and finally flung to the earth with a crash. The big dog lay still as a log.

A sense of fear born of the knowledge of impotence came over Scarlett; what in the name of evil did it all mean? The smart scientist had no faith in the occult, and yet what *did* it all mean?

Nobody stirred. Scarlett's companions were soaked and soddened with fatigue; the rolling thunder of artillery would have scarce disturbed them. With teeth set and limbs that trembled, Scarlett crawled over to the dog.

The great, black-muzzled creature was quite dead. The full chest was stained and soaked in blood; the throat had been cut apparently with some jagged, saw-like instrument away to the bone. And, strangest thing of all, scattered all about the body was a score or more of the great purple orchid flowers broken off close to the head. A hot, pricking sensation travelled slowly up Scarlett's spine and seemed to pass out at the tip of his skull. He felt his hair rising.

He was frightened. As a matter of honest fact, he had never been so horribly scared in his life before. The whole thing was so mysterious, so cruel, so blood-thirsty.

Still, there must be some rational explanation. In some way the matter had to do with the purple orchid. The flower had an evil reputation. Was it not known to these Cubans as the devil's poppy?

Scarlett recollected vividly now Zara's white, scared face when Tito had volunteered to show the way to the resplendent bloom; he remembered the cry of the girl and the blow that followed. He could see it all now. The girl had meant to warn him against some nameless horror to which Tito was leading the small party. This was the jealous Cuban's revenge.

A wild desire to pay this debt to the uttermost fraction filled Scarlett, and shook him with a trembling passion. He crept along in the drenching dew to where Tito lay, and touched his forehead with the chill blue rim of a revolver barrel. Tito stirred slightly.

"You dog!" Scarlett cried. "I am going to shoot you."

Tito did not move again. His breathing was soft and regular. Beyond a doubt the man was sleeping peacefully. After all he might be innocent; and yet, on the other hand, he might be so sure of his quarry that he could afford to slumber without anxiety as to his vengeance.

In favour of the latter theory was the fact that the Cuban lay beyond the limit of what had previously been the circle of dry bones. It was just possible that there was no danger outside that pale. In that case it would be easy to arouse the rest, and so save them from the horrible death which had befallen the mastiff. No doubt these were a form of upas tree, but that would not account for the ghastly spectacle in mid-air.

"I'll let this chap sleep for the present," Scarlett muttered. He crawled back, not without misgivings, into the ring of death. He meant to wake the others and then wait for further developments. By now his senses were more alert and vigorous than they had ever been before. A preternatural clearness of brain and vision possessed him. As he advanced he saw suddenly falling a green bunch of cord that straightened into a long, emerald line. It was triangular in shape, fine at the apex, and furnished with hooked spines. The rope appeared to dangle from the tree overhead; the broad, sucker-like termination was evidently soaking up moisture.

A natural phenomenon evidently, Scarlett thought. This was some plant new to him, a parasite living amongst the tree-tops and drawing life and vigour by means of these green, rope-like antennae designed by Nature to soak and absorb the heavy dews of night.

For a moment the logic of this theory was soothing to Scarlett's distracted nerves, but only for a moment, for then he saw at regular intervals along the green rope the big purple blossoms of the devil's poppy.

He stood gasping there, utterly taken aback for the moment. There must be some infernal juggling behind all this business. He saw the rope slacken and quiver, he saw it swing forward like a pendulum, and the next minute it had passed across the shoulders of a sleeping seaman.

Then the green root became as the arm of an octopus. The line shook from end to end like the web of an angry spider when invaded by a wasp. It seemed to grip the sailor and tighten, and then, before Scarlett's afrighted eyes, the sleeping man was raised gently from the ground.

Scarlett jumped forward with a desire to scream hysterically. Now that a comrade was in danger he was no longer afraid. He whipped a jack-knife from his pocket and slashed at the cruel cord. He half expected to meet with the stoutness of a steel strand, but to his surprise the feeler snapped like a carrot, bumping the sailor heavily on the ground.

He sat up, rubbing his eyes vigorously.

"That you, sir?" he asked. "What is the matter?"

"For the love of God, get up at once and help me to arouse the others," Scarlett said, hoarsely. "We have come across the devil's workshop. All the horrors of the inferno are invented here."

The bluejacket struggled to his feet. As he did so, the clothing from his waist downwards slipped about his feet, clean cut through by the teeth of the green parasite. All around the body of the sailor blood oozed from a zone of teeth-marks.

Two-o'clock-in-the-morning courage is a virtue vouchsafed to few. The tar, who would have faced an ironclad cheerfully, fairly shivered with fright and dismay.

"What does it mean, sir?" he cried. "I've been—"

"Wake the others," Scarlett screamed; "wake the others."

Two or three more green tangles of rope came tumbling to the ground, straightening and quivering instantly. The purple blossoms stood out like a frill upon them. Like a madman, Scarlett shouted, kicking his companions without mercy.

They were all awake at last, grumbling and moaning for their lost slumbers. All this time Tito had never stirred.

"I don't understand it at all," said Tarrer.

"Come from under those trees," said Scarlett, "and I will endeavour to explain. Not that you will believe me for a moment. No man can be expected to believe the awful nightmare I am going to tell you."

Scarlett proceeded to explain. As he expected, his story was followed with marked incredulity, save by the wounded sailor, who had strong evidence to stimulate his otherwise defective imagination.

"I can't believe it," Tarrer said, at length. They were whispering together beyond earshot of Tito, whom they had no desire to arouse for obvious reasons. "This is some diabolical juggling of yonder rascally Cuban. It seems impossible that those slender green cords could—"

Scarlett pointed to the centre of the circle.

"Call the dog," he said grimly, "and see if he will come."

"I admit the point as far as the poor old mastiff is concerned. But at the same time I don't—however, I'll see for myself."

By this time a dozen or more of the slender cords were hanging pendent from the trees. They moved from spot to spot as if jerked up by some unseen hand and deposited a foot or two farther. With the great purple bloom fringing the stem, the effect was not unlovely save to Scarlett, who could see only the dark side of it. As Tarrer spoke he advanced in the direction of the trees.

"What are you going to do?" Scarlett asked.

"Exactly what I told you. I am going to investigate this business for myself."

Without wasting further words Scarlett sprang forward. It was no time for the niceties of an effete civilization. Force was the only logical argument to be used in a case like this, and Scarlett was the more powerful man of the two.

Tarrer saw and appreciated the situation.

"No, no," he cried; "none of that. Anyway, you're too late."

He darted forward and threaded his way between the slender emerald columns. As they moved slowly and with a certain stately deliberation there was no great danger to an alert and vigorous individual. As Scarlett entered the avenue he could hear the soak and suck as the dew was absorbed.

"For Heaven's sake, come out of it," he cried.

The warning came too late. A whip-like trail of green touched Tarrer from behind, and in a lightning flash he was in the toils. The tendency to draw up anything and everything gave the cords a terrible power. Tarrer evidently felt it, for his breath came in great gasps.

"Cut me free," he said, hoarsely; "cut me free. I am being carried off my feet."

He seemed to be doomed for a moment, for all the cords there were apparently converging in his direction. This, as a matter of fact, was a solution of the whole sickening, horrible sensation. Pulled here and there, thrust in one direction and another, Tarrer contrived to keep his feet.

Heedless of possible danger to himself Scarlett darted forward, calling to his companions to come to the rescue. In less time than it takes to tell, four knives were at work ripping and slashing in all directions.

"Not all of you," Scarlett whispered. So tense was the situation that no voice was raised above a murmur. "You two keep your eyes open for fresh cords, and cut them as they fall, instantly. Now then."

The horrible green spines were round Tarrer's body like snakes. His face was white, his breath came painfully, for the pressure was terrible. It seemed to Scarlett to be one horrible dissolving view of green, slimy cords and great weltering, purple blossoms. The whole of the circle was strewn with them. They were wet and slimy underfoot.

Tarrer had fallen forward half unconscious. He was supported now by but two cords above his head. The cruel pressure had been relieved. With one savage sweep of his knife Scarlett cut the last of the lines, and Tarrer fell like a log unconscious to the ground. A feeling of nausea, a yellow dizziness, came over Scarlett as he staggered beyond the dread circle. He saw Tarrer carried to a place of safety, and then the world seemed to wither and leave him in the dark.

"I feel a bit groggy and weak," said Tarrer an hour or so later: "but beyond that this idiot of a Richard is himself again. So far as I am concerned, I should like to get even with our friend Tito for this."

"Something with boiling oil in it," Scarlett suggested, grimly. "The callous scoundrel has slept soundly through the whole of this business. I suppose he felt absolutely certain that he had finished with us."

"Upon my word, we ought to shoot the beggar," Tarrer exclaimed.

"I have a little plan of my own," said Scarlett, "which I am going to put in force later on. Meanwhile we had better get on with breakfast. When Tito wakes a pleasant little surprise will await him."

Tito roused from his slumbers in due course and looked around him. His glance was curious, disappointed, then full of a white and yellow fear. A thousand conflicting emotions streamed across his dark face. Scarlett read them at a glance as he called the Cuban over to him.

"I am not going into any unnecessary details with you," he said. "It has come to my knowledge that you are playing traitor to us. Therefore we prefer to complete our journey alone. We can easily find the way now."

"The señor may do as he pleases," he replied. "Give me my dollar and let me go."

Scarlett replied grimly that he had no intention of doing anything of the kind. He did not propose to place the lives of himself and his comrades in the power of a rascally Cuban who had played false.

"We are going to leave you here till we return," he said. "You will have plenty of food, you will be perfectly safe under the shelter of these trees, and there is no chance of anybody disturbing you. We are going to tie you up to one of these trees for the next four-and-twenty hours."

All the insolence died out of Tito's face. His knees bowed, a cold dew came out over the ghastly green of his features. From the shaking of his limbs he might have fared disastrously with ague.

"The trees," he stammered, "the trees, señor! There is danger from snakes, and—and from many things. There are other places—"

"If this place was safe last night it is safe to-day," Scarlett said, grimly. "I have quite made up my mind."

Tito fought no longer. He fell forward on his knees, he howled for mercy, till Scarlett fairly kicked him up again.

"Make a clean breast of it," he said, "or take the consequences. You know perfectly well that we have found you out, scoundrel."

Tito's story came in gasps. He wanted to get rid of the Americans. He was jealous. Besides, under the Americanos would Cuba be any better off? By no means and assuredly not. Therefore it was the duty of every good Cuban to destroy the Americanos where possible.

"A nice lot to fight for," Scarlett muttered. "Get to the point."

Hastened to the point by a liberal application of stout shoe-leather, Tito made plenary confession. The señor himself had suggested death by medium of the devil's poppies. More than one predatory plant-hunter had been lured to his destruction in the same way. The skeleton hung on the tree was a Dutchman who had walked into the clutch of the purple terror innocently. And Pierre Anton had done the same. The suckers of the devil's poppy only came down at night to gather moisture; in the day they were coiled up like a spring. And anything that they touched they killed. Tito had watched more than one bird or small beast crushed and mauled by these cruel spines with their fringe of purple blossoms.

"How do you get the blooms?" Scarlett asked.

"That is easy," Tito replied. "In the daytime I moisten the ground under the trees. Then the suckers unfold, drawn by the water. Once the suckers unfold one cuts several of them off with long knives. There is danger, of course, but not if one is careful."

"I'll not trouble the devil's poppy any further at present," said Scarlett, "but I shall trouble you to accompany me to my destination as a prisoner."

Tito's eyes dilated.

"They will not shoot me?" he asked, hoarsely.

"I don't know," Scarlett replied. "They may hang you instead. At any rate, I shall be bitterly disappointed if they don't end you one way or the other. Whichever operation it is, I can look forward to it with perfect equanimity."

Writer and political activist Edith Nesbit is chiefly remembered today for her fine children's books, but she wrote several excellent weird tales, including the classic "Man-Size in Marble." She also co-founded, with her husband Hume Bland, the Fabian Party, a precursor to the modern Labour Party. "The Pavilion" first appeared in the November 1915 issue of The Strand.

THE PAVILION

E. NESBIT

THERE WAS NEVER a moment's doubt in her own mind. So she said afterwards. And everyone agreed that she had concealed her feelings with true womanly discretion. Her friend and confidant, Amelia Davenant, was at any rate completely deceived. Amelia was one of those featureless blondes who seem born to be overlooked. She adored her beautiful friend, and never, from first to last, could see any fault in her, except, perhaps, on the evening when the real things of the story happened. And even in that matter she owned at the time that it was only that her darling Ernestine did not understand.

Ernestine was a prettyish girl with the airs, so irresistible and misleading, of a beauty; most people said that she was beautiful, and she certainly managed, with extraordinary success, to produce the illusion of beauty. Quite a number of plainish girls achieve that effect nowadays. The freedom of modern dress and coiffure and the increasing confidence in herself which the modern girl experiences, aid her in fostering the illusion; but in the sixties, when everyone wore much the same sort of bonnet, when your choice in coiffure was limited to bandeaux or ringlets, and the crinoline was your only wear, something very like genius was needed to deceive the world in the matter of your personal charms. Ernestine had that genius; hers was the smiling, ringletted, dark-haired, dark-eyed, sparkling type.

Amelia had blond bandeaux and kind appealing blue eyes, rather too small and rather too dull; her hands and ears were beautiful, and she kept them out of sight as much as possible. In our times the blond hair would have been puffed out to make a frame for the forehead, a little too high; a certain shade of blue and a certain shade of boldness would have her eyes effective. And the beautiful hands would have learned that flower-like droop of the wrist so justly and so universally admired. But as it was, Amelia was very nearly plain, and in her secret emotional self-communings told herself that she was ugly. It was she who, at the age of fourteen, composed the remarkable poem beginning:

> *I know that I am ugly: did I make*
> *The face that is the laugh and jest of all?*

—And goes on, after disclaiming any personal responsibility for the face, to entreat the kind earth to "cover it away from mocking eyes," and to "let the daisies blossom where it lies."

Amelia did not want to die, and her face was not the laugh and jest, or indeed the special interest, of anyone. All that was poetic license. Amelia had read perhaps a little too much poetry of "*Quand je suis morte, mes amies, plantez un saule au cimetière*"; but really life was a very good thing to Amelia, especially when she had a new dress and someone paid her a compliment. But she went on writing verses extolling the advantages of The Tomb, and grovelling metrically at the feet of One who was Another's until that summer, when she was nineteen, and went to stay with Ernestine at Doricourt. Then her Muse took flight, scared, perhaps, by the possibility, suddenly and threateningly presented, of being asked to inspire verse about the real things of life. At any rate, Amelia ceased to write poetry about the time when she and Ernestine and Ernestine's aunt went on a visit to Doricourt, where Frederick Powell lived with his aunt. It was not one of those hurried motor-fed excursions which we have now, and call week-ends, but a long leisurely visit, when all the friends of the static aunt called on the dynamic aunt, and both returned the calls with much state, a big barouche and a pair of fat horses. There were croquet parties and archery parties and little dances, all pleasant informal little gaieties arranged without ceremony among people who lived within driving distance of each other and knew each other's tastes and incomes and family history as well as they knew their own. The habit of importing huge droves of strangers from distant counties for brief harrying raids did not then obtain. There was instead a wide and constant circle of pleasant people with an unflagging stream of gaiety, mild indeed, but delightful to unjaded palates.

And at Doricourt life was delightful even on the days when there was no party. It was perhaps more delightful to Ernestine than to her friend, but even so, the one least pleased was Ernestine's aunt.

"I do think," she said to the other aunt whose name was Julia— "I daresay it is not so to you, being accustomed to Mr. W. Frederick, of course, from his childhood, but I always find gentlemen in the house so unsettling, especially young gentlemen, and when there are young ladies also. One is always on the *qui vive* for excitement."

"Of course," said Aunt Julia, with the air of a woman of the world; "living as you and dear Ernestine do, with only females in the house...."

"We hang up an old coat and hat of my brother's on the hatstand in the hall," Aunt Emmeline protested.

"...The presence of gentlemen in the house must be a little unsettling. For myself, I am inured to it. Frederick has so many friends. Mr. Thesiger, perhaps, the greatest. I believe him to be a most worthy young man, but peculiar." She leaned forward across her bright-tinted Berlin woolwork and spoke impressively, the needle with its trailing red poised in air. "You know, I hope you will not think it indelicate of me to mention such a thing, but dear Frederick....your dear Ernestine would have been in every way so suitable."

"Would have been?" Aunt Emmeline's tortoise-shell shuttle ceased its swift movement among the white loops and knots of her tatting.

"Well, my dear," said the other aunt, a little shortly, "you must surely have noticed...."

"You don't mean to suggest that Amelia...I thought Mr. Thesiger and Amelia...."

"Amelia! I really must say! No, I was alluding to Mr. Thesiger's attentions to dear Ernestine. Most marked. In dear Frederick's place I should have found some excuse for shortening Mr. Thesiger's visit. But, of course, I cannot interfere. Gentlemen must manage these things for themselves. I only hope that there will be none of that trifling with the most holy affections of others which...."

The less voluable aunt cut in hotly with: "Ernestine's incapable of anything so unladylike."

"Just what I was saying," the other rejoined blandly, got up and drew the blind a little lower, for the afternoon sun was glowing on the rosy wreaths of the drawing-room carpet.

Outside in the sunshine Frederick was going his best to arrange his own affairs. He had managed to place himself beside Miss Ernestine Meutys on the stone steps of the pavilion; but then, Mr. Thesiger lay along the lower step at her feet, a very good position for looking up into her eyes. Amelia was beside him, but then it never seemed to matter whom Amelia sat beside.

They were talking about the pavilion on whose steps they sat, and Amelia who often asked uninteresting questions had wondered how old it was. It was Frederick's pavilion after all, and he felt this when his friend took the words out of his mouth and used them on his own account, even though he did give the answer in the form of an appeal.

"The foundations are Tudor, aren't they?" he said. "Wasn't it an observatory or laboratory or something of that sort in Fat Henry's time?"

"Yes," said Frederick, "there was some story about a wizard or an alchemist or something, and it was burned down, and then they rebuilt it in its present style."

"The Italian style, isn't it?" said Thesiger; "but you can hardly see what it is now, for the creeper."

"Virginia creeper, isn't it?" Amelia asked, and Frederick said: "Yes, Virginia creeper." Thesiger said it looked more like a South American plant, and Ernestine said Virginia was in South America and that was why. "I know, because of the war," she said modestly, and nobody smiled or answered. There were manners in those days.

"There's a ghost story about it surely," Thesiger began again, looking up at the dark closed doors of the pavilion.

"Not that I ever heard of," said the pavilion's owner. "I think the country people invented the tale because there have always been so many rabbits and weasels and things found dead near it. And once a dog, my uncle's favourite spaniel. But of course that's simply because they get entangled in the Virginia creeper—you see how fine and big it is—and can't get out, and die as they do in traps. But the villagers prefer to think it's ghosts."

"I thought there was a real ghost story," Thesiger persisted.

Ernestine said: "A ghost story. How delicious! Do tell it, Mr. Doricourt. This is just the place for a ghost story. Out of doors and the sun shining, so that we can't really be frightened."

Doricourt protested again that he knew no story.

"That's because you never read, dear boy," said Eugene Thesiger. "That library of yours. There's a delightful book—did you never notice it?—brown tree calf with your arms on it; the head of the house writes the history of the house as far as he knows it. There's a lot in that book. It began in Tudor times—1515 to be exact."

"Queen Elizabeth's time," Ernestine thought that made it so much more interesting. "And was the ghost story in that?"

"It isn't exactly a ghost story," said Thesiger. "It's only that the pavilion seems to be an unlucky place to sleep in."

"Haunted?" Frederick asked, and added that he must look up that book.

"Not haunted exactly. Only several people who have slept the night there went on sleeping."

"Dead, he means," said Ernestine, and it was left for Amelia to ask:

"Does the book tell anything particular about how the people died? What killed them, or anything?"

"There are suggestions," said Thesiger; "but there, it is a gloomy subject. I don't know why I started it. Should we have time for a game of croquet before tea, Doricourt?"

"I wish *you'd* read the book and tell me the stories," Ernestine said to Frederick, apart, over the croquet balls.

"I will," he answered fervently, "you've only to tell me what you want."

"Or perhaps Mr. Thesiger will tell us another time—in the twilight. Since people like twilight for ghosts. Will you, Mr. Thesiger?" She spoke over her blue muslin shoulder.

Frederick certainly meant to look up the book, but he delayed till after supper; the half-hour before bed when he and Thesiger put on their braided smoking-jackets and their braided smoking-caps with the long yellow tassels, and smoked the cigars which were, in those days still, more of a luxury than a necessity. Ordinarily, of course, these were smoked out of doors, or in the smoking-room, a stuffy little den littered with boots and guns and yellow-backed railway novels. But to-night Frederick left his friend in that dingy hutch, and went alone to the library, found the book and took it to the circle of light made by the colza lamp.

"I can skim through it in half an hour," he said, and wound up the lamp and lighted his second cigar. Then he opened the shutters and windows, so that the room should not smell of smoke in the morning. Those were the days of consideration for the ladies who had not yet learned that a cigarette is not exclusively a male accessory like a beard or a bass voice.

But when, his preparations completed, he opened the book, he was compelled to say "Pshaw!" Nothing short of this could relieve his feelings. (You know the expression I mean, though of course it isn't pronounced as it's spelt, any more than Featherstonehaugh or St. Maur are.)

"Pshaw!" said Frederick, fluttering the pages. His remark was justified. The earlier part of the book was written in the beautiful script of the early sixteenth century, that looks so plain and is so impossible to read, and the later pages, though the handwriting was clear and Italian enough, left Frederick helpless, for the language was Latin, and Frederick's Latin was limited to the particular passages he had "been through" at his private school. He recognised a word here and there, *mors*, for instance, and *pallidus* and *pavor* and *arcanum*, just as you or I might; but to read the complicated stuff and make sense of it...! Frederick said something just a shade stronger than "Pshaw!" —"Botheration!" I think it was; replaced the book on the shelf, closed the shutters and turned out the lamp. He thought he would ask Thesiger to translate the thing, but then again he thought he wouldn't. So he went to bed wishing that he had happened to remember more of the Latin so painfully beaten into the best years of his boyhood.

And the story of the pavilion was, after all, told by Thesiger.

There was a little dance at Doricourt next evening, a carpet dance, they called it. The furniture was pushed back against the walls, and the tightly stretched Axminster carpet was not so bad to dance on as you might suppose. That, you see, was before the days of polished floors and large rugs with loose edges that you can catch your feet in. A carpet was a carpet in those days, well and truly laid, conscientiously exact to the last least recess and fitting the floor like a skin. And on this quite tolerable surface the young people danced very happily, some ten or twelve couples. The old people did not dance in those days, except sometimes a quadrille of state to "open the ball." They played cards in a room provided for the purpose, and in the dancing-room three or four kindly middle-aged ladies were considered to provide ample chaperonage. You were not even expected to report yourself to your chaperon at the conclusion of a dance. It was not like a real ball. And even in those far-off days there were conservatories.

It was on the steps of the conservatory, not the steps leading from the dancing-room, but the steps leading to the garden, that the story was told. The four young people were sitting together, the girls' crinolined flounces spreading round them like huge pale roses, the young men correct in their high-shouldered coats and white cravats. Ernestine had been very kind to both the men—a little too kind, perhaps, who can tell? At any rate, there was in their eyes exactly that light which you may imagine in the eyes of rival stags in the mating season. It was Ernestine who asked Frederick for the story, and Thesiger who, at Amelia's suggestion, told it.

"It's quite a number of stories," he said, "and yet it's really all the same story. The first man to sleep in the pavilion slept there ten years after it was built. He was a friend of the alchemist or astrologer who built it. He was found dead in the morning. There seemed to have been a struggle. His arms bore the marks of cords. No; they never found any cords. He died from loss of blood. There were curious wounds. That was all the rude leeches of the day could report to the bereaved survivors of the deceased."

"How funny you are, Mr. Thesiger," said Ernestine with that celebrated soft low laugh of hers. When Ernestine was elderly, many people thought her stupid. When she was young, no one seems to have been of this opinion.

"And the next?" asked Amelia.

"The next was sixty years later. It was a visitor that time, too. And he was found dead with just the same marks, and the doctors said the same thing. And so it went on. There have been eight deaths altogether—unexplained deaths. Nobody has slept in it now for over a hundred years. People seem to have a prejudice against the place as a sleeping apartment. I can't think why."

"Isn't he simply killing?" Ernestine asked Amelia, who said:

"And doesn't anyone know how it happened?" No one answered till Ernestine repeated the question in the form of: "I suppose it was just accident?"

"It was a curiously recurrent accident," said Thesiger, and Frederick, who throughout the conversation had said the right things at the right moment, remarked that it did not do to believe all these old legends. Most old families had them, he believed. Frederick had inherited Doricourt from an unknown great-uncle of whom in life he had not so much as heard, but he was very strong on the family tradition. "I don't attach any importance to these tales myself."

"Of course not. All the same," said Thesiger deliberately, "you wouldn't care to pass a night in that pavilion."

"No more would you," was all Frederick found on his lips.

"I admit that I shouldn't enjoy it," said Eugene, "but I'll bet you a hundred you don't *do* it."

"Done," said Frederick.

"Oh, Mr. Doricourt," breathed Ernestine, a little shocked at betting "before ladies."

"Don't!" said Amelia, to whom, of course, no one paid any attention, "don't do it."

You know how, in the midst of flower and leafage, a snake will suddenly, surprisingly rear a head that threatens? So, amid friendly talk and laughter, a sudden fierce antagonism sometimes looks out and vanishes again, surprising most of all the antagonists. This antagonism spoke in the tones of both men, and after Amelia had said, "Don't," there was a curiously breathless little silence. Ernestine broke it. "Oh," she said, "I do wonder which of you will win. I should like them both to win, wouldn't you, Amelia? Only I suppose that's not always possible, is it?"

Both gentlemen assured her that in the case of bets it was very rarely possible.

"Then I wish you wouldn't," said Ernestine. "You could *both* pass the night there, couldn't you, and be company for each other? I don't think betting for such large sums is quite the thing, do you, Amelia?"

Amelia said No, she didn't, but Eugene had already begun to say:

"Let the bet be off then, if Miss Meutys doesn't like it. That suggestion is invaluable. But the thing itself needn't be off. Look here, Doricourt. I'll stay in the pavilion from one to three and you from three to five. Then honour will be satisfied. How will that do?"

The snake had disappeared.

"Agreed," said Frederick, "and we can compare impressions afterwards. That will be quite interesting."

Then someone came and asked where they had all got to, and they went in and danced some more dances. Ernestine danced twice with Frederick and drank iced sherry and water and they said good-night and lighted their bedroom candles at the table in the hall.

"I do hope they won't," Amelia said as the girls sat brushing their hair at the two large white muslin frilled dressing-tables in the room they shared.

"Won't what?" said Ernestine, vigorous with the brush.

"Sleep in that hateful pavilion. I wish you'd ask them not to, Ernestine. They'd mind, if *you* asked them."

"Of course I will if you like, dear," said Ernestine cordially. She was always the soul of good nature. "But I don't think you ought to believe in ghost stories, not really."

"Why not?"

"Oh, because of the Bible and going to church and all that," said Ernestine. "Do you really think Rowland's Macassar has made any difference to my hair?"

"It is just as beautiful as it always was," said Amelia, twisting up her own little ashen-blond handful. "What was that?"

That was a sound coming from the little dressing-room. There was no light in that room. Amelia went into the little room though Ernestine said: "Oh, don't! how can you? It might be a ghost or a rat or something," and as she went she whispered: "Hush!"

The window of the little room was open and she leaned out of it. The stone sill was cold to her elbows through her print dressing-jacket.

Ernestine went on brushing her hair. Amelia heard a movement below the window and listened. "To-night will do," someone said"

"It's too late," said someone else.

"If you're afraid, it will always be too late or too early," said someone. And it was Thesiger

"You know I'm not afraid," the other one, who was Doricourt, answered hotly.

"An hour for each of us will satisfy honour," said Thesiger carelessly. "The girls will expect it. I couldn't sleep. Let's do it now and get it over. Let's see. Oh, damn it!"

A faint click had sounded.

"Dropped my watch. I forgot the chain was loose. It's all right though; glass not broken even. Well, are you game?"

"Oh, yes, if you insist. Shall I go first, or you?"

"I will," said Thesiger. "That's only fair, because I suggested it. I'll stay till half-past one or a quarter to two, and then you come on. See?"

"Oh, all right. I think it's silly, though," said Frederick.

Then the voices ceased. Amelia went back to the other girl.

"They're going to do it to-night."

"Are they, dear?" Ernestine was placid as ever. "Do what?"

"Sleep in that horrible pavilion."

"How do you know?"

Amelia explained how she knew.

"Whatever can we do?" she added.

"Well, dear, suppose we go to bed," suggested Ernestine helpfully. "We shall hear all about it in the morning."

"But suppose anything happens?"

"What could happen?"

"Oh, *anything*," said Amelia. "Oh, I do wish they wouldn't! I shall go down and ask them not to."

"*Amelia*" the other girl was at last aroused. "You *couldn't*. I shouldn't *let* you dream of doing anything so unladylike. What would the gentlemen think of you?"

The question silenced Amelia, but she began to put on her so lately discarded bodice.

"I won't go if you think I oughtn't," she said.

"Forward and fast, auntie would call it," said the other. "I am almost sure she would."

"But I'll keep dressed. I shan't disturb you. I'll sit in the dressing-room. I *can't* go to sleep while he's running into this awful danger."

"Which he?" Ernestine's voice was very sharp. "And there isn't any danger."

"Yes, there is," said Amelia sullenly, "and I mean *them*. Both of them."

Ernestine said her prayers and got into bed. She had put her hair in curl-papers which became her like a wreath of white roses.

"I don't think auntie will be pleased," she said, "when she hears that you sat up all night watching young gentlemen. Good-night, dear!"

"Good-night, darling," said Amelia. "I know you don't understand. It's all right. "

She sat in the dark by the dressing-room window. There was no moon, but the starlight lay gray on the dew of the park, and the trees massed themselves in bunches of a darker gray, deepening to black at the roots of them. There was no sound to break the stillness, except the little cracklings of twigs and rustlings of leaves as birds or little night wandering beasts moved in the shadows of the garden, and the sudden creakings that furniture makes if you sit alone with it and listen in the night's silence.

Amelia sat on and listened, listened. The pavilion showed in broken streaks of pale grey against the wood that seemed to be clinging to it in dark patches. But that, she reminded herself, was only the creeper. She sat there for a very long time, not knowing how long a time it was. For anxiety is a poor chronometer, and the first ten minutes had seemed an hour. She had no watch. Ernestine had—and slept with it under her pillow. The stable clock was out of order; the man had been sent for to see to it. There was nothing to measure time's flight by, and she sat there rigid, straining her ears for a foot-fall on the grass, straining her eyes to see a figure come out of the dark pavilion and across the dew-grey grass towards the house. And she heard nothing, saw nothing.

Slowly, imperceptibly, the grey of the sleeping trees took on faint dreams of colour. The sky turned faint above the trees, the moon perhaps was coming out. The pavilion grew more clearly visible. It seemed to Amelia that something moved along the leaves that surrounded it, and she looked to see him come out. But he did not come.

"I wish the moon would really shine," she told herself. And suddenly she knew that the sky was clear and that this growing light was not the moon's cold shiver, but the growing light of dawn.

She went quickly into the other room, put her hand under the pillow of Ernestine, and drew out the little watch with the diamond "E" on it.

"A quarter to three," she said aloud. Ernestine moved and grunted.

There was no hesitation about Amelia now. Without another thought for the ladylike and the really suitable, she lighted her candle and went quickly down the stairs, paused a moment in the hall, and so out through the front door. She passed along the terrace. The feet of Frederick protruded from the open French window of the smoking-room. She set down her candle on the terrace—it burned clearly enough in that clear air—went up to Frederick as he slept, his head between his shoulders and his hands loosely hanging, and shook him.

"Wake up," she said, —"Wake up! Something's happened! It's a quarter to three and he's not come back."

"Who's not what?" Frederick asked sleepily.

"Mr. Thesiger. The pavilion."

"Thesiger?—the ...*You*, Miss Davenant? I beg your pardon. I must have dropped off."

He got up unsteadily, gazing dully at this white apparition still in evening dress with pale hair now no longer wreathed.

"What is it?" he said. "Is anybody ill?"

Briefly and very urgently Amelia told him what it was, implored him to go at once and see what had happened. If he had been fully awake, her voice and her eyes would have told him many things.

"He said he'd come back," he said. "Hadn't I better wait? You go back to bed, Miss Davenant. If he doesn't come in half an hour...."

"If you don't go this minute," said Amelia tensely, "I shall."

"Oh, well, if you insist," Frederick said. "He has simply fallen asleep as I did. Dear Miss Davenant, return to your room, I beg. In the morning when we are all laughing at this false alarm, you will be glad to remember that Mr. Thesiger does not know of your anxiety."

"I hate you," said Amelia gently, "and I am going to see what has happened. Come or not, as you like." She caught up the silver candlestick and he followed its wavering gleam down the terrace steps and across the grey dewy grass.

Half-way she paused, lifted the hand that had been hidden among her muslin flounces and held it out to him with a big Indian dagger in it.

"I got it out of the hall," she said. "If there's any real danger. Anything living, I mean. I thought...But I know I couldn't use it. Will you take it?"

He took it, laughing kindly.

"How romantic you are," he said admiringly and looked at her standing there in the mingled gold and grey of dawn and candlelight. It was as though he had never seen her before.

They reached the steps of the pavilion and stumbled up them. The door was closed but not locked. And Amelia noticed that the trails of creeper had not been disturbed, they grew across the doorway, as thick as a man's finger, some of them.

"He must have got in by one of the windows," Frederick said. "Your dagger comes in handy, Miss Davenant."

He slashed at the wet sticky green stuff and put his shoulder to the door. It yielded at a touch and they went in.

The one candle lighted the pavilion hardly at all, and the dusky light that oozed in through the door and windows helped very little. And the silence was thick and heavy.

"Thesiger!" said Frederick, clearing his throat. "Thesiger! Hullo! Where are you?"

Thesiger did not say where he was. And then they saw.

There were low seats to the windows, and between the windows low stone benches ran. On one of these something dark, something dark and in places white, confused the outline of the carved stone.

"Thesiger," said Frederick again in the tone a man uses to a room that he is almost sure is empty. "Thesiger!"

But Amelia was bending over the bench. She was holding the candle crookedly so that it flared and guttered.

"Is he there?" Frederick asked, following her; "is that him? Is he asleep?"

"Take the candle," said Amelia, and he took it obediently. Amelia was touching what lay on the bench. Suddenly she screamed. Just one scream, not very loud. But Frederick remembers just how it sounded. Sometimes he hears it in dreams and wakes moaning, though he is an old man now and his old wife says: "What is it, dear?" and he says: "Nothing, my Ernestine, nothing."

Directly she had screamed she said: "He's dead," and fell on her knees by the bench. Frederick saw that she held something in her arms.

"Perhaps he isn't," she said. "Fetch someone from the house, brandy—send for a doctor. Oh, go, go, go!"

"I can't leave you here," said Frederick with thoughtful propriety; "suppose he revives?"

"He will not revive," said Amelia dully, "go, go, go! Do as I tell you. Go! If you don't go," she added suddenly and amazingly, "I believe I shall kill you. It's all your doing."

The astounding sharp injustice of this stung Frederick into action.

"I believe he's only fainted or something," he said. "When I've roused the house and everyone has witnessed your emotion you will regret...."

She sprang to her feet and caught the knife from him and raised it, awkwardly, clumsily, but with keen threatening, not to be mistaken or disregarded. Frederick went.

When Frederick Came back, with the groom and the gardener (he hadn't thought it well to disturb the ladies), the pavilion was filled full of white revealing daylight. On the bench lay a dead man, and kneeling by him a living woman on whose warm breast his cold and heavy head lay pillowed. The dead man's hands were full of the green crushed leaves, and thick twining tendrils were about his wrists and throat. A wave of green seemed to have swept from the open window to the bench where he lay.

The groom and the gardener and the dead man's friend looked and looked.

"Looks like as if he'd got himself entangled in the creeper and lost 'is 'ead," said the groom, scratching his own.

"How'd the creeper get in, though? That's what I says," it was the gardener who said it.

"Through the window," said Doricourt, moistening his lips with his tongue.

"The window was shut, though, when I come by at five yesterday," said the gardener stubbornly. " 'Ow did it get all that way since five?"

They looked at each other, voicing, silently, impossible things.

The woman never spoke. She sat there in the white ring of her crinolined dress like a broken white rose. But her arms were round Thesiger and she would not move them.

When the doctor came, he sent for Ernestine who came, flushed and sleepy-eyed and very frightened, and shocked.

"You're upset, dear," she said to her friend, "and no wonder. How brave of you to come out with Mr. Doricourt to see what happened. But you can't do anything now, dear. Come in and I'll tell them to get you some tea."

Amelia laughed, looked down at the face on her shoulder, laid the head back on the bench among the drooping green of the creeper, stooped over it, kissed it and said quite quietly and gently: "Good-bye, dear, good-bye!"—took Ernestine's arm and went away with her.

The doctor made an examination and gave a death certificate. "Heart failure," was his original and brilliant diagnosis. The certificate said nothing, and Frederick said nothing, of the creeper that was wound about the dead man's neck, nor of the little white wounds, like little bloodless lips half-open, that they found about the dead man's neck.

"An imaginative or uneducated person," said the doctor, "might suppose that the creeper had something to do with his death. But we mustn't encourage superstition. I will assist my man to prepare the body for its last sleep. Then we need not have any chattering woman."

"Can you read Latin?" Frederick asked. The doctor could, and, later, did.

It was the Latin of that brown book with the Doricourt arms on it that Frederick wanted read. And when he and the doctor had been together with the book between them for three hours, they closed it, and looked at each other with shy and doubtful eyes.

"It can't be true," said Frederick.

"If it is," said the more cautious doctor, "you don't want it talked about. I should destroy that book if I were you. And I should root up that creeper and burn it. It is quite evident, from what you tell me, that your friend believed that this creeper was a man-eater, that it fed, just before its flowering time, as the book tells us, at dawn; and that he fully meant that the thing when it crawled into the pavilion seeking its prey should find you and not him. It would have been so, I understand, if his watch had not stopped at one o'clock."

"He dropped it, you know," said Doricourt like a man in a dream.

"All the cases in this book are the same," said the doctor, "the strangling, the white wounds. I have heard of such plants; I never believed." He shuddered. "Had your friend any spite against you? Any reason for wanting to get you out of the way?"

Frederick thought of Ernestine, of Thesiger's eyes on Ernestine, of her smile at him over her blue muslin shoulder.

"No," he said, "none. None whatever. It must have been accident. I am sure he did not know. He could not read Latin." He lied, being, after all, a gentleman, and Ernestine's name being sacred.

"The creeper seems to have been brought here and planted in Henry the Eighth's time. And then the thing began. It seems to have been at its flowering season that it needed the... that, in short, it was dangerous.

The little animals and birds found dead near the pavilion.... But to move itself all that way, across the floor! The thing must have been almost conscient," he said with a sincere shudder. "One would think," he corrected himself at once, "that it knew what it was doing, if such a thing were not plainly contrary to the laws of nature."

"Yes," said Frederick, "one would. I think if I can't do anything more I'll go and rest. Somehow all this has given me a turn. Poor Thesiger!"

His last thought before he went to sleep was one of pity.

"Poor Thesiger," he said; "how violent and wicked! And what an escape for me! I must never tell Ernestine. And all the time there was Amelia.... Ernestine would never have done *that* for *me*." And on a little pang of regret for the impossible he fell asleep.

Amelia went on living. She was not the sort that dies even of such a thing as happened to her on that night, when for the first and last time she held her love in her arms and knew him for the murderer he was. It was only the other day that she died, a very old woman. Ernestine who, beloved and surrounded by children and grandchildren, survived her, spoke her epitaph:

"Poor Amelia," she said, "nobody ever looked the same side of the road where she was. There was an indiscretion when she was young. Oh, nothing disgraceful, of course. She was a lady. But people talked. It was the sort of thing that stamps a girl, you know."

Like his more famous contemporary, M. R. James, Ulric Daubeny was an antiquarian and writer of supernatural tales, most of which were collected as The Elemental *(London: Routledge, 1919). "The Sumach," reprinted from that volume, is an effective and unusual tale reminiscent of an earlier James story. Daubeny's career ended far too quickly, when the writer was struck down by meningitis at age 34.*

THE SUMACH

ULRIC DAUBENY

"HOW RED THAT SUMACH IS!"

Irene Barton murmured something commonplace, for to her the tree brought painful recollections. Her visitor, unconscious of this fact, proceeded to elaborate.

"Do you know, Irene, that tree gives me the creeps! I can't explain, except that it is not a nice tree, not a *good* tree. For instance, why should its leaves be red in August, when they are not supposed to turn until October?"

"What queer ideas you have, May! The tree is right enough, although its significance to me is sad. Poor Spot, you know; we buried him beneath it two days ago. Come and see his grave."

The two women left the terrace, where this conversation had been taking place, and leisurely strolled across the lawn, at the end of which, in almost startling isolation, grew the Sumach. At least, Mrs Watcombe, who evinced so great an interest in the tree, questioned whether it actually was a Sumach, for the foliage was unusual, and the branches gnarled and twisted beyond recognition. Just now, the leaves were stained with splashes of dull crimson, but rather than droop, they had a bloated appearance, as if the luxuriance of the growth were not altogether healthy.

For several moments they stood regarding the pathetic little grave, and the silence was only broken when Mrs Watcombe darted beneath the tree, and came back with something in her hand.

"Irene, look at this dead thrush. Poor little thing! Such splendid plumage, yet it hardly weighs a sugar plum!"

Mrs Barton regarded it with wrinkled brows.

"I cannot understand what happens to the birds, May—unless someone lays poison. We continually find them dead about the garden, and usually beneath, or very near this tree.

It is doubtful whether Mrs Watcombe listened. Her attention seemed to wander that morning, and she was studying the twisted branches of the Sumach with a thoughtful scrutiny.

"Curious that the leaves should turn at this time of year," she murmured. "It brings to mind poor Geraldine's illness. This tree had an extraordinary fascination for her, you know. It was quite scarlet then, yet that was only June, and it had barely finished shooting."

"My dear May! You have red leaves on the brain this morning!" Irene retorted, uncertain whether to be irritated or amused. "I can't think why you are so concerned about the colour. It is only the result of two days' excessive heat, for scarcely a leaf was touched, when I buried poor old Spot."

The conversation seemed absurdly trivial, yet, Mrs Watcombe gone, Irene could not keep her mind from dwelling on her cousin's fatal illness. The news had reached them with the shock of the absolutely unexpected. Poor Geraldine, who had always been so strong, to have fallen victim to acute anaemia! It was almost unbelievable, that heart failure should have put an end to her sweet young life, after a few days' ailing. Of course, the sad event had wrought a wonderful change for Irene and her husband, giving them, in place of a cramped suburban villa, this beautiful country home, Cleeve Grange. Everything for her was filled with the delight of novelty, for she had ruled as mistress over the charmed abode for only one short week. Hilary, her husband, was yet a stranger to the more intimate of its attractions, being detained in London by the winding-up of business affairs.

Several days elapsed, for the most part given solely to the keen pleasure of arranging and re-arranging the new home. As time went by, the crimson splashes on the Sumach faded, the leaves becoming green again, though drooping as if from want of moisture. Irene noticed this when she paid her daily visits to the pathetic little dog grave, trying to induce flowers to take root upon it, but do what she might, they invariably faded. Nothing, not even grass, would grow beneath the Sumach. Only death seemed to thrive there, she mused in a fleeting moment of depression, as she searched around for more dead birds. But none had fallen since the thrush, picked up by Mrs Watcombe.

One evening, the heat inside the house becoming insupportable, Irene wandered into the garden, her steps mechanically leading her to the little grave beneath the Sumach. In the uncertain moonlight, the twisted trunk and branches of the old tree were suggestive of a rustic seat, and feeling tired, she lifted herself into the natural bower, and lolled back, joyously inhaling the cool night air. Presently she dropped asleep, and in a curiously vivid manner, dreamt of Hilary; that he had completed his business in London, and was coming home. They met at evening, near the garden gate, and Hilary spread wide his arms, and eagerly folded them about her. Swiftly the dream began to change, assuming the characteristic of a nightmare. The sky grew strangely dark, the arms fiercely masterful, while the face which bent to kiss her neck was not that of her young husband: it was leering, wicked, gnarled like the trunk of some weather-beaten tree. Chilled with horror, Irene fought long and desperately against the vision, to be at last awakened by her own frightened whimpering. Yet returning consciousness did not immediately dissipate the nightmare. In imagination she was still held rigid by brutal arms, and it was only after a blind, half-waking struggle that she freed herself, and went speeding across the lawn, towards the lighted doorway.

Next morning Mrs Watcombe called, and subjected her to a puzzled scrutiny.

"How pale you look Irene. Do you feel ill?"

"Ill! No, only a little languid. I find this hot weather very trying."

Mrs Watcombe studied her with care, for the pallor of Irene's face was very marked. In contrast, a vivid spot of red showed on the slender neck, an inch or so below the ear. Intuitively a hand went up, as Irene turned to her friend in explanation.

"It feels so sore. I think I must have grazed the skin, last night, while sitting in the Sumach."

"Sitting in the Sumach!" echoed Mrs Watcombe in surprise. "How curious you should do that. Poor Geraldine used to do the same, just before she was taken ill, and yet at the last she was seized with a perfect horror of the tree. Goodness, but it is quite red again, this morning!"

Irene swung round in the direction of the tree, filled with a vague repugnance. Sure enough, the leaves no longer drooped, nor were they green. They had become flecked once more with crimson, and the growth had quite regained its former vigour.

"Eugh!" she breathed, hurriedly turning towards the house. "It reminds me of a horrid nightmare. I have rather a head this morning; let's go in, and talk of something else!"

As the day advanced, the heat grew more oppressive, and night brought with it a curious stillness, the stillness which so often presages a heavy thunderstorm. No bird had offered up its evening hymn, no breeze came sufficient to stir a single leaf: everything was pervaded by the silence of expectancy.

The interval between dinner and bedtime is always a dreary one for those accustomed to companionship, and left all alone, Irene's restlessness momentarily increased. First the ceiling, then the very atmosphere seemed to weigh heavy upon her head. Although windows and doors were all flung wide, the airlessness of the house grew less and less endurable, until from sheer desperation she made her escape into garden, where a sudden illumination of the horizon gave warning of the approaching storm. Feeling somewhat at a loss, she roamed aimlessly awhile, pausing sometimes to catch the echoes of distant thunder, until at last she found herself standing over Spot's desolate little grave. The sight struck her with a sense of utter loneliness, and tears sprang to her eyes, in poignant longing for the companionship of her faithful pet.

Moved by she knew not what, Irene swung herself into the comfortable branches of the old Sumach, and soothed by the reposeful attitude, her head soon began to nod in slumber. Afterwards it was a doubtful memory whether she actually did sleep, or whether the whole experience was not a kind of waking nightmare. Something of the previous evening's dream returned to her, but this time with added horror; for it commenced with no pleasurable vision of her husband. Instead, relentless, stick-like arms immediately closed in upon her, their vice-like grip so tight that she could scarcely breathe. Down darted the awful head, rugged and lined by every sin, darting at the fair, white neck as a wild beast on its prey. The foul lips began to eat into her skin.... She struggled desperately, madly, for to her swooning senses the very branches of the tree became endowed with active life, coiling unmercifully around her, tenaciously clinging to her limbs, and tearing at her dress. Pain at last spurred her to an heroic effort, the pain of something—perhaps a twig—digging deep into her unprotected neck. With a choking cry she freed herself, and nerved by a sudden burst of thunder, ran tottering towards the shelter of the house.

Having gained the cosy lounge-hall, Irene sank into an armchair, gasping hysterically for breath. Gusts of refreshing wind came through the open windows, but although the atmosphere rapidly grew less stagnant, an hour passed before she could make sufficient effort to crawl upstairs to bed. In her room, a further shock awaited her. The bloodless, drawn face reflected in the mirror was scarcely recognizable. The eyes lacked lustre, the lips were white, the skin hung flabby on the shrunken flesh, giving it a look of premature old age. A tiny trickle dry blood, the solitary smudge of colour, stained the chalky pallor of her neck. Taking up a hand-glass, she examined this with momentary concern. It was the old wound reopened, an angry-looking sore, almost like the bite of some small, or very sharp-toothed, animal. It smarted painfully....

Mrs Watcombe, bursting into the breakfast room next morning, with suggestions of an expedition to the neighbouring town, was shocked at Irene's looks, and insisted on going at once to fetch the doctor. Mrs Watcombe fussed continually throughout the interview, and insisted on an examination of the scar upon Irene's neck. Patient and doctor had regarded this as a negligible detail, but finally the latter subjected it to a slightly puzzled scrutiny, advising that it should be kept bandaged. He suggested that Irene was suffering from anaemia and would do well to keep as quiet as possible, building up her strength with food, open windows and a general selection of pills and tonics. But despite these comforting arrangements, no one was entirely satisfied. The doctor lacked something in assurance, Irene was certain that she could not really be anaemic, while Mrs Watcombe was obsessed by inward misgivings, perfectly indefinable, yet none the less disturbing. She left the house as a woman bent under a load of care. Passing up the lane, her glance lighted on the old Sumach, more crimson now, more flourishing in its growth than she had seen it since the time of Geraldine's fatal illness.

"I loathe that horrid old tree!" she murmured, then added, struck by a nameless premonition, "Her husband ought to know. I shall wire to him at once."

Irene, womanlike, put to use her enforced idleness, by instituting a rearrangement of the box-room, the only part of her new home which yet remained unexplored. Among the odds and ends of the rubbish to be thrown away, there was a little notebook, apparently unused. In idle curiosity, Irene picked it up, and was surprised to learn, from an inscription, that her cousin Geraldine had intended to use it as a diary. A date appeared—only a few days prior to the poor girl's death—but no entries had been made, though the first two pages of the book had certainly been removed. As Irene put it down, there fluttered to the ground a torn scrap of writing. She stooped, and continued stooping, breathlessly staring at the words that had been written by her cousin's hand—*Sumach fascinates m*——

In some unaccountable manner this applied to her. It was obvious what tree was meant, the old Sumach at the end of the lawn; and it fascinated her, Irene, though not until that moment had she openly recognized the fact. Searching hurriedly through the notebook, she discovered, near the end, a heap of torn paper, evidently the first pages of a diary. She turned the pieces in eager haste. Most of them bore no more than one short word, or portions of a longer one, but a few bigger fragments proved more enlightening, and filled with nervous apprehension, she carried the book to her escritoire, and spent the remainder of the afternoon in trying to piece together the torn-up pages.

Meanwhile, Mrs Watcombe was worrying and fretting over Irene's unexpected illness. Her pallor, her listlessness, even the curious mark upon her neck, gave cause for positive alarm, so exactly did they correspond with symptoms exhibited by her cousin Geraldine, during the few days prior to her death. She wished that the village doctor, who had attended the earlier case, would return soon from his holiday, as his locum tenens seemed sadly wanting in that authoritative decision which is so consoling to patients, relatives, and friends. Feeling, as an old friend, responsible for the welfare of Irene, she wired to Hilary, telling him of the sudden illness, and advising him to return without delay.

The urgency of the telegram alarmed him, so much so that he left London by the next train, arriving at Cleeve Grange shortly after dark.

"Where is your mistress?" was his first enquiry, as the maid met him in the hall.

"Upstairs, Sir. She complained of feeling tired, and said she would go to bed."

He hurried to her room, only to find it empty. He called, he rang for the servants; in a moment the whole house was astir, yet nowhere was Irene to be found. Deeming it possible that she might have gone to see Mrs

Watcombe, Hilary was about to follow, when that lady herself was ushered in.

"I saw the lights of your cab—" she commenced, cutting short the sentence, as she met his questioning glance.

"Where is Irene?"

"Irene? My dear Hilary, is she not here?"

"No. We can't find her anywhere. I thought she might have been with you."

For the space of half a second, Mrs Watcombe's face presented a picture of astonishment; then the expression changed to one of dismayed concern.

"She is in that tree! I'm certain of it! Hilary, we must fetch her in at once!"

Completely at a loss to understand, he followed the excited woman into the garden, stumbling blindly in her wake across the lawn. The darkness was intense; and a terrific wind beat them back as if with living hands. Irene's white dress at length became discernible, dimly thrown up against the pitchy background, and obscured in places by the twists and coils of the old Sumach. Between them they grasped the sleeping body, but the branches swung wildly in the gale, and to Hilary's confused imagination it was as if they had literally to tear it from the tree's embrace. At last they regained the shelter of the house, and laid their inanimate burden upon the sofa. She was quite unconscious, pale as death, and her face painfully contorted, as if with fear. The old wound on the neck, now bereft of bandages, had been reopened, and was wet with blood.

Hilary rushed off to fetch the doctor, while Mrs Watcombe and the servants carried Irene to her room. Several hours passed before she recovered consciousness, and during that time Hilary was gently but firmly excluded from the sickroom. Bewildered and disconsolate, he wandered restlessly about the house, until his attention was arrested by the unusual array of torn-up bits of paper on Irene's desk. He saw that she had been sorting out the pieces, and sticking them together as the sentences became complete. The work was barely half finished, yet what there was to read, struck him as exceedingly strange:

> The seat in the old Sumach fascinates me. I find myself going back to it unconsciously, nay, even against my will. Oh, but the nightmare visions it always brings me! In them I seem to plumb the very depths of terror. Their memory preys upon my mind, and every day my strength grows less.
> Dr H. speaks of anaemia....

That was as far as Irene had proceeded. Hardly knowing why he did so, Hilary resolved to complete the task, but the chill of early morning was in the air before it was finished. Cramped and stiff, he was pushing back his chair when a footstep sounded in the doorway, and Mrs Watcombe entered.

"Irene is better," she volunteered immediately. "She is sleeping naturally, and Doctor Thomson says there is no longer any immediate danger. The poor child is terribly weak and bloodless."

"May—tell me—what is the meaning of all this? Why has Irene suddenly become so ill? I can't understand it!"

Mrs Watcombe's face was preternaturally grave.

"Even the doctor admits that he is puzzled," she answered very quietly. "The symptoms all point to a sudden and excessive loss of blood, though in cases of acute anaemia—

"God! But—not like Geraldine? I can't believe it!"

"Neither can I. Oh, Hilary, you may think me mad, but I can't help feeling that there is some unknown, some awful influence at work. Irene was perfectly well three days ago, and it was the same with Geraldine before she was taken ill. The cases are so exactly similar…Irene was trying to tell me something about a diary, but the poor girl was too exhausted to make herself properly understood."

"Diary? Geraldine's diary, do you think? She must mean that. I have just finished piecing it together, but frankly, I can't make head or tail of it!"

Mrs Watcombe rapidly scanned the writing, then studied it again with greater care. Finally she read the second part aloud.

"Listen, Hilary! This seems to me important."

Dr H. speaks of anaemia. Pray heaven, he may be correct, for my thoughts sometimes move in a direction which foreshadows nothing short of lunacy—or so people would tell me, if I could bring myself to confide these things. I must fight alone, clinging to the knowledge that it is usual for anaemic persons to be obsessed by unhealthy fancies. If only I had not read those horribly suggestive words in Barrett….

"Barrett? What can she mean, May?"

"Wait a moment. Barrett? Barrett's *Traditions of the County*, perhaps. I have noticed a copy in the library. Let us go there; it may give the clue!" The book was quickly found, and a marker indicated the passage to which Geraldine apparently referred.

At Cleeve, I was reminded of another of those traditions, so rapidly disappearing before the spread of education. It concerned the old belief in vampires, spirits of the evil dead, who by night, could assume a human form, and scour the countryside in search of victims. Suspected vampires, if caught, were buried with the mouth stuffed full of garlic, and a stake plunged through the heart, whereby they were rendered harmless, or, at least, confined to that one particular locality.

Some thirty years ago, an old man pointed out a tree which was said to have grown from such a stake. So far as I can recollect, it was an unusual variety of Sumach, and had been enclosed during a recent extension to the garden of the old Grange....

"Come outside," said Mrs Watcombe, breaking a long and solemn silence. "I want you to see that tree."

The sky was suffused with the blush of early dawn, and the shrubs, the flowers, even the dew upon the grass caught and reflected something of the pink effulgence. The Sumach alone stood out, dark and menacing. During the night its leaves had become a hideous, mottled purple; its growth was oily, bloated, unnaturally vigorous, like that of some rank and poisonous weed.

Mrs Watcombe, looking from afar, spoke in frightened, husky tones.

"See, Hilary! It was exactly like that when—when Geraldine died!"

When evening fell, the end of the lawn was strangely bare. In place of the old tree, there lay an enormous heap of smouldering embers—enormous, because the Sumach had been too sodden with dark and sticky sap, to burn without the assistance of large quantities of other timber.

Many weeks elapsed before Irene was sufficiently recovered to walk as far as Spot's little grave. She was surprised to find it almost hidden in a bed of garlic.

Hilary explained that it was the only plant they could induce to grow there.

Other books from Dead Letter Press:

THE MYSTERIOUS FLAME *by Orrin Grey* **OUT OF PRINT**
(Limited-edition softcover chapbook, January 2009)

ENGELBRECHT AGAIN! *by Rhys Hughes*
(Limited-edition hardcover, October 2008)

THE KING OF DEADTOWN *by Glynn Barrass* **OUT OF PRINT**
(Limited-edition softcover chapbook, March 2008)

BOUND FOR EVIL: CURIOUS TALES OF BOOKS GONE BAD
edited by Tom English (Limited-edition hardcover, January 2008)
OUT OF PRINT

PHANTASMAPEDIA *by Mark McLaughlin* **OUT OF PRINT**
(Limited-edition softcover chapbook, November 2007)

BLOOD COVEN *by Christopher Fulbright & Angeline Hawkes*
(Limited-edition softcover chapbook, May 2007) **OUT OF PRINT**

DEAD LETTER PRESS
BOX 134 NEW KENT, VA 23124-0134
www.DeadLetterPress.com

THE LITERARY VAMPIRE SERIES *edited by Tom English*
(These are the titles of the original series, issued as limited-edition
softcover chapbooks, May 2005-2009) **ALL ARE OUT OF PRINT.**

CLASSIC VAMPIRES REVISITED: THE BLOODY ROOTS
CLASSIC VAMPIRES REVISITED: DARK SUCKLINGS
CLASSIC VAMPIRES REVISITED: LENORA
THE VAMPYRE: A TALE *by Dr. John Polidori*
CLASSIC VAMPIRES REVISITED: BLACK SUNDAY
CLASSIC VAMPIRES REVISITED: A BEGUILING CORRUPTION
CLASSIC VAMPIRES REVISITED: RED SCARE
THE MYSTERIOUS STRANGER *by Anonymous*
THE LAST LORDS OF GARDONAL *by William Gilbert*
CARMILLA *by Joseph Sheridan Le Fanu*
CLASSIC VAMPIRES REVISITED: A GROWING FEAR
CLASSIC VAMPIRES REVISITED: A CONSUMING PASSION
CLASSIC VAMPIRES REVISITED: AN UNEASY REPOSE
CLASSIC VAMPIRES REVISITED: A RIPENING EVIL
IN THE DWELLINGS OF THE WILDERNESS *by C. Bryson Taylor*
THE HOUSE OF THE VAMPIRE *by George Sylvester Viereck*
CLASSIC VAMPIRES REVISITED: A SHOCKING REVELATION
CLASSIC VAMPIRES REVISITED: A HARVEST OF HORROR
CLASSIC VAMPIRES REVISITED: A FEARFUL FEASTING
CLASSIC VAMPIRES REVISITED: AND STILL WE HUNGER
CLASSIC VAMPIRES REVISITED: A BOTANICAL NIGHTMARE
THE KISS OF JUDAS & THE DEATH OF HALPIN FRAYSER
CLASSIC VAMPIRES REVISITED: A MORBID FASCINATION
THE VAMPIRE IN LITERATURE *by Montague Summers*